MW01713115

Jimmy's Love Story

A NOVEL

For my gentle care giver, Debby —
(no "ouches").
With thanks, John

Jimmy's Love Story

A NOVEL

JOHN McCURDY

TWOHARBORS

Two Harbors Press
212 3rd Avenue North, Suite 290
Minneapolis, MN 55401
612.455.2293
www.TwoHarborsPress.com

ISBN - 978-1-936198-45-0
ISBN - 1-936198-45-2
LCCN - 2010930486

Cover Design and Typeset by Melanie Shellito

Printed in the United States of America

To Kathy for her challenge to do it right.

ACKNOWLEDGEMENTS:

My profound gratitude to Jackie Ball for coaching, believing in the story, and inspiring the re-writes.

Many thanks to Joni Aveni and Jean Devine for their encouragement, smart editing, and positive plot advice.

And, much appreciation to my brother, Joe, who said he loved it from the start!

CHAPTER ONE

"Mommy's over here, Daddy! Look, we go by the little angel."

Mike Flynn had been counting off the rows of headstones in the East Lawn Cemetery and looked up, startled, to see his four-year-old son angling down an aisle toward the still-fresh grave. *I promised her I'd take care of him,* he thought, *but he's already looking after me.*

"Good for you, Jimmy. Let's go together." Jimmy waited for his father to catch up and take his hand. He was proud he had found the way, but now he wasn't eager to get there first. "Ah, Jimmy, Mommy always loved roses, remember?" Jimmy leaned into his father as they got to her grave and Mike crouched next to him, arm around Jimmy as they both bent to place the roses on the metal name-plate. "What prayer today?" Mike asked. "The Hail Mary?"

"Let's say my goodnight prayer, Daddy. I'll start."

"Dear Lord, Thank you for this lovely day
And everything that in it lay.
For rest and food and loving care
And all that makes the world so fair."

The lump came back fast in Mike's throat and chest as his son started the prayer, and he had to cough harshly to get control. Tears came anyway, but he was able to join Jimmy with the rest of the words.

"Help me to do the things I should,
To be to others kind and good.
In all I do and all I say
To grow more loving every day. Amen."

"When will Mommy's stone come, Daddy?"

The thin brass grave marker was just pegged into the ground and Jimmy was worried it would be lost somehow.

Marie Rose Flynn
3/6/61-4/10/95
Requiescat In Pacem

"Don't worry, Jimmy. It takes time to carve all the letters in and make the stone shiny. Here, let's clean up some of these dead flowers." *God, this doesn't get any easier*, Mike thought as they gathered up stems and petals from the flowers that had given up since last Sunday. Mike had stopped by nearly every day since Marie had been buried three weeks earlier, but this was just the second visit for Jimmy. Like the week before, they had been to the nine-thirty a.m. Mass at St. Vincent De Paul Church, which was a short, three block drive from the East Lawn Cemetery in East Haven, Connecticut.

Mike married Marie Rose Torelli in that church. It was where she had been baptized, made her First Communion and had been confirmed. Where she and her two younger sisters had grown up. And now, just thirty-four years later, St. Vincent was where Marie had been sent home to God.

Fran and Thomas Torelli, Marie's parents, still lived in East Haven with Marie's two younger sisters, Carmen and Regina. Fran and Thomas had been to the Mass which Mike and Jimmy had just attended, but because they knew Mass was a prelude to a cemetery visit, they avoided their usual pew and sat in the back of the church to give their son-in-law and grandson time and space for themselves and their sorrow.

Now, as Mike and Jimmy were bagging the debris they had picked up, Fran and Thomas were rolling their car to a stop behind Mike's fairly new Honda Accord, a company car from WJS-TV Channel 5, New Haven, for whom Mike sold advertising time. The Torellis were driving a four-year-old Ford Taurus, because Fran didn't like taking Thomas's flashy red Cadillac Coupe de Ville to church.

Mike was relieved to see them, because a short visit would make it easier for Jimmy and him to leave Marie behind. Besides, Jimmy was the real pet in the family and knew it.

"Maman!" Jimmy squealed. "Papa!" His short legs launched him a few steps down the path until he cut diagonally to intercept his grandparents and almost slipped in the slick, fresh, April grass. Fran gasped as Thomas swept him into an arc that terminated seven feet above the lawn, in shrieks of joy from Jimmy and whoops of "atta boys" from Thomas.

"Down you go," said Thomas. "Here, give me a kiss." He hugged Jimmy to his car coat.

"Maman, here's *your* big hug and a kiss," Jimmy said, dodging out of Papa's hug. He was mimicking Maman's favorite expression of affection and earned a huge grin and squeal of delight from her. She bent to one knee to cuddle him in her arms and snuggle her face in his neck.

"Mom. Dad. This is great," said Mike. "I should have called you. We were just at the nine-thirty."

"We saw you, Mike," Fran said. "We knew you wanted a few minutes alone with Marie."

How could she know that these quiet, generous feelings would cause tears to well up simultaneously in both of them?

"Oh, Mike, how about a hug for me?" Mike wrapped his arms about her in an embrace that really said *I love you*.

"Jimmy," Thomas called, "let's take a walk to the pond. We can see some goldfish if we're lucky."

Mike caught Thomas's eye and nodded. Turning to Fran he said, "Mom, I'm getting back to work this week, and I'm wondering how much of Jimmy's stuff he should bring with him."

"We can't take Jimmy, Mike." Fran caught her breath and took a half step back from him, bracing herself for his reaction.

"What do you mean, Mom? What do you mean take him? You and Marie and Thomas and I weren't talking 'taking'; we were talking watching him during the day. What's this you can't take him? You can't watch him? What am I going to do?" Mike abruptly checked himself, surprised at the vehemence of his reaction. He could still recall his wife's last glow of nearly her last smile when he had promised her Jimmy would be okay. Then softly he said, "What is it, Fran?"

"Mike, I'm sorry. We've been talking about it and it just won't work. I'm so sorry, Mike." Tears again welled up in Fran's eyes. She had promised Marie and Mike, and Thomas had supported her, but they just couldn't do it. "Look, we could help with money for day care..."

"Money? Money's not the issue, Fran. Love's the issue. Jimmy needs love—all day long. And I need to know he's getting love. You can't buy love." He turned away from her in sudden anger over his unspeakable disappointment.

"Mike, please." Fran reached out to touch his arm, and Mike startled her by jerking away. "We'll give all the love we have. We just don't have the time every day."

"Jimmy, come on back." Mike's voice sounded harsher than he intended. Then, "We'll be late, Jimmy. We've got to go."

Jimmy sensed at once that something wasn't right, and as his face turned a deep red, he stood stock still, and fresh tears rose and streaked down his cheeks. Mike was proud of him, as he knelt at his son's side, that Jimmy had not started bawling. *He's acting the man*, thought Mike. And aloud, "It's all right, my man. I've just got some work to do at home."

"But I can stay, Daddy. Maman and Papa will take care of me. And Carmen or Regina can take me home later."

"No, Jimmy. Maman and Papa have things they have to do too. We're all disappointed but that's it. So time for kisses."

"Maman," Jimmy cried. And now he started to really cry—not like the stoic soldier-personality he had just exhibited. "Maman, tell Daddy you'll take care of me today."

At this, Fran herself couldn't help bursting into tears—some of sheer love and regret but most because of the shame she felt. The effect of this was to double Jimmy's grief, and he cried all the louder as Thomas stepped in to console the two of them. He knelt to be at eye level with Jimmy but still put an arm around Fran's waist.

"That's it, Jimmy. No more crying," Mike said. "You're a big boy and you promised." He tried to sound like an understanding father but there was a certain edge to his voice that forced a wail of despair from his son. "What *is* it, Jimmy?" Mike knelt himself and put his hands around Jimmy's waist, drawing the boy to him and away from his grandfather.

"I promised Fluffy, Daddy. You remember." Mike did remember and jerked his head up, recalling Jimmy's bedtime decision last night about his favorite nighttime friend. Fluffy had been Jimmy's companion from his crib days, and last night Jimmy had decided he wanted to leave Fluffy at his mother's grave. This was a brave way to suddenly become more than a toddler, but Mike's heart had ached at the enormity of the decision. By itself, leaving Fluffy would be hard enough, but after this disappointment it would be far worse. "Please, Daddy. Fluffy's in the car keeping warm, and if I stay for a while with Maman and Papa maybe Fluffy won't be afraid so much." The words rushed out, and Mike could see that Fran and Thomas were struck by Jimmy's intention.

"Mike," Fran said, "I think it's better if we do it Jimmy's way." She was grateful for Jimmy's decision, which now forced a softer resolution to the bitter exchange between her and Mike.

"Is it okay, Daddy?" Mike nodded, and Jimmy shrieked with joy and bounded back to the car for Fluffy.

"Fran told me," Mike said to Thomas. "I don't understand what's going on, but I guess you've got your reasons. It's going to be tough."

Thomas looked down and just shrugged as if twice defeated. He looked much older than fifty-four, Mike thought. "I'm sorry," he said.

Embarrassed for him, Mike turned abruptly to Fran. "Jimmy will need help with Fluffy I think. Since he seems to be counting on you, is it okay to ask you to help him through this?"

Fran nodded. "Of course, Mike. Don't think what I said before means it's all over for us. We're still family. Jimmy's still our blood, and you're still our son-in-law. We love both of you."

"Yeah, well." Mike couldn't figure it out.

"One of the girls will bring him back right after lunch," Fran said. "Say, one or two o'clock."

"Fluffy's all set," said Jimmy, scampering back to them. "I brought his blanket too."

"You sure you want to do this, Jimmy? Right?" Mike said. "Fluffy may go straight up to heaven too, you know." Mike was thinking about some jerk picking up the forlorn little stuffed animal.

"This is how Fluffy gets to heaven—to see Mommy again. You have to go, Daddy. Maman and Papa will take care of me." Jimmy stepped up to his father for a strong loving squeeze and a kiss.

Mike pulled on Jimmy's ear—an odd expression of affection, but one they both knew was just between the two of them. Jimmy responded with the obligatory ouch and Mike countered by tweaking the other ear. "See you later, Daddy," Jimmy said.

Mike couldn't bring himself to thank his puzzling in-laws, so he raised a hand in a gesture of appreciation and said he would expect Jimmy by two o'clock. Then he turned and walked quickly back to his car. On the way, he watched for and located the little angel that Jimmy used as his marker. *You're quite a guy, young man*, he thought. And then he heaved a great sigh, and tears started pouring from his eyes.

After starting the car, he drove about a hundred yards around a bend and gave into paroxysms of heaving, mournful, beseeching, and finally, self-pitying sobs. He was completely out of control for two, three minutes—it seemed much longer—then started up and looked about, abashed. And seeing no one, he felt sudden freedom—sudden release. Finally, he was able to get through the huge outpouring that his priest had encouraged and warned about. And he finally felt some of his usual restraint, able to go on and move forward and think and do for Jimmy and himself. *Well,* he thought. *So that's it. You get a whack in the head. You wake up. You move on. Now I've got to figure it out.*

He started the car and moved briskly up through the gates, turned right onto Coe Avenue, and made his way onto Interstate 95 south. Back to New Haven.

CHAPTER TWO

Almost immediately, the southbound traffic came to a dead stop, and Mike was able to see that his three lanes of traffic were parked on the "Q" bridge, which spanned the Quinnipiac River. This meant an accident at the far side of the bridge was blocking both I-95 south and the exit to northbound I-91 to Hartford. Too bad, because if either option were open Mike could have taken alternate routes home. But he was used to lost time on this bridge. For years it became backed up for no obvious reason, and no one, including federal experts, could figure out how to keep traffic moving. *So what,* he thought, as he eased down the windows to let the on-shore breeze from Long Island Sound whisper fresh sea smells through his windows. Following the relief of his catharsis at the cemetery, he was content to have some slow time to consider next steps.

Glancing at the dashboard digital, he was surprised to see it was almost eleven-thirty. No wonder he could feel the familiar ache. Mike's job involved a lot of lunchtime and dinnertime entertainment, and despite current convention of one glass of white wine or just seltzer and lime, Mike's choices of beverage always included cocktails or beer or wine—or all three. "So, if that's okay during the week—conducting business—it should be doubly okay on weekends—conducting relaxation." Mike said this aloud, and it certainly sounded reasonable to him. In the days when Marie would caution him about his excess, Mike would try to shrug the blame off on his Irish heritage. When Marie pressed, Mike would start on, "All the wine you Italians like to put away. I've heard it's up to a gallon a day. Ha, ha, ha." He knew his logic was transparent though, and was grateful Marie usually let it go.

Now he realized he was about a quarter mile from an exit and then just ten lights and five minutes through spotty Sunday traffic to his second floor, railroad apartment in a Whitney Avenue brownstone. He could drive the Honda down the adjacent alley, park in the back, and scamper up to the apartment to drop Jimmy's stuff and check any phone messages, then skip two blocks west, one block south and stroll through the door of Phelan's Pub just in time to quiet his ache—if the traffic would start to move.

And it did. When he saw the usually slow, right-hand lane moving, he decided to head north a tenth of a mile on I-91, cut through Little Italy's Wooster Street, bounce out on Orange, and intercept Whitney in less than five minutes. *Yes*, he thought. *Touchdown!*

There had been no calls, and the freezer produced a frozen chicken Parmesan, which he took out to defrost for Jimmy's and his dinner later on. He tugged off his tie, replaced his sports jacket with a sweater, and headed out to Phelan's. It was just minutes past noon, and Jimmy would probably not be back until one-thirty, easily. This would give him time for a few beers and time to think about Jimmy.

"Mike," shouted the bartender, Tim Halloran, "I'd given you up for dead. Where you been?" He grinned his wide, goofy smile and flipped three pasteboard beer coasters at Mike, one after the other, pelting him in the chest and shoulder as Mike tried fruitlessly to catch them. You never duck one of Tim's shots.

"I stopped at the Broadway Bar on my way," Mike said, "but the ladies there were too refined, so I had to settle for this dump. If you've got the spigots turned on yet you can draw me an Elm City—plenty of head. And just in time, too!"

Over the next hour, Mike downed two more draughts while the bar welcomed another dozen regulars, some bringing friends or dates, so that a friendly hum of talk and laughter filled the place. Tim owned Phelan's, and his wife, Heather, made cold cut sandwiches, waited tables, told jokes, and mainly kept a sober eye out for patrons who weren't. She asked Mike, "Who's looking after Jimmy today?"

"Oh, the in-laws will be dropping him off in a bit. In time for our afternoon naps," Mike said. "When are you gonna dump that wife-beater of yours and sail off with me to parts unknown?" he asked with his irrepressible grin.

Heather snapped her towel at his elbow, grinned back and said, "How about a sandwich, sailor? Is baloney okay?"

Mike finished the sandwich, dropped some money on the bar, and left Phelan's, giving pats on the shoulders to his friends at the bar. As he went up the street to his address, he could see Carmen and Jimmy just getting out of the Torellis' Cadillac, and he whistled to attract their attention. He was high, and he felt good about it.

"Daddy," shrilled Jimmy. "We just got here, and Carmen went eighty miles an hour. It was cool—we passed everyone!"

"Carmen?" Mike lifted his eyebrows at his sister-in-law and, winking, she said, "I think we set a new speed record for the trip from East Haven...a fantastic thirty minutes. But it sure seemed fast, didn't it, Jimmy?"

Mike caught on and bent to scoop up his exhilarated son. "How about we take a couple naps? What do you say, Jimmy?" Then, "Thanks for getting him home, Carmen. How's school?"

"Can't wait to get it over with. Are you coming to graduation next month?" Carmen knew he would be but used this to avoid asking the platitudinous, *how're you doing*?

"We'll be there," said Mike. "Thanks again."

Jimmy extended his arms to hug his aunt goodbye. Mike thanked

Carmen. She said, "See you next week, I guess," and waved over her shoulder as she drove off in the flashy sedan.

Mike awoke at three-thirty, quickly showered, looked in on Jimmy, and decided to leave him curled into a tight little ball for another hour or so. What Mike needed was a solution to the weekday caring of his son, and he realized there weren't many options. His parents still lived just outside Boston in Wellesley, far too distant to even think about it. Besides, they both were in their sixties and long out of practice with youngsters, even if they would be willing.

His father, Michael James Flynn, an only child, had been born in 1928—the year before the market crashed—into a family that never really suffered from the economic reprisals of the depression. They weren't well off at all; they really were dirt poor, but his grandfather, Aloysius "Mac" Flynn, had been a ward organizer in Boston for the entrenched Irish political forces. He was fifty years old when Mike was born, and old and smart enough to know how to look poor while pocketing big money and still taking good care of his ward and the mayor. He'd been the patriarch at Mike's 1988 wedding to Marie, and lived another four years with all his faculties and simply died in his sleep at eighty-five years old. *Who could ask for more*? Mike thought. "Mac" Flynn had set up his own son, Mike's dad, in a job as a news reporter for the *Boston Herald*.

Mike's grandmother, born Meagan Walsh, was a wonderful, doting Nana who pre-deceased her husband by six or seven years, and in Mike's memory was just a wonderful, old-fashioned gal who had rocked him when young, and taught him an old Irish prayer or two. Mike was twenty-nine when she died, two years before his marriage to Marie. Wonderful folks, but no match for the heritage on his mother's side of the family.

The youngest of five privileged siblings, Gail Standish Flynn was the aristocratic daughter of Charles W. Standish and Barbara Woods of Boston's Beacon Hill. A crusty Episcopalian, Charles was near seventy when his daughter, Gail, married Mike's dad, and he simply hadn't the resistance to protest this unseemly match with a Roman Catholic. His wife, "Nanny Baba," on the other hand, about fifteen years younger than he, was euphoric over the Catholic (Flynn)—Protestant(Standish) union since, as a strayed Catholic herself, she felt a felicitous sense of redemption. Because of the family's silk stocking connections, his mother had been hired as a society reporter at the *Herald,* which is where she met and fell in love with Mike's Dad. He had joined the Navy in 1945, the day after he graduated from high school, and hadn't seen much more of the world than the Boston Navy Yard. But the GI bill helped put him through school (Boston College, of course), and he loved learning about Boston society while accompanying his girl, then fiancée, then wife, to her job's obligatory soirees. They had married in 1953, and Mike's older sister, Mary Standish Flynn, was born two years later.

Mike often thought about how Mary had reflected their mother's "debutante" upbringing and had always been a prim, proper, well-spoken representative of Boston Brahmins. She graduated from Radcliffe College in Cambridge after studying elementary education, but intended to marry well as soon as she could.

On the other hand, Mike didn't have much time for dainty, watercress sandwiches and tea. He shouldered his way through his growing-up years, picking up some even rougher edges than his dad and mystifying his mother. Naturally, this studied lack of refinement embarrassed his older sister, who was reluctant to even acknowledge him when her friends were around. Mike took extraordinary delight in surprising her with a bear hug when she was unsuspecting and lifting and twirling her so that her friends had to scatter. "I hate you! I hate you!" she would scream at him as he and his equally boorish pals sauntered away.

Now Mike was thinking hard about the possibility that Mary would be willing to care for Jimmy. She had achieved her goal of marrying well and lived about an hour north in Farmington, Connecticut with her husband and their two daughters, Barbara, fifteen years old, and Martha, who would be fourteen in July. Their father, Mary's prize catch, Thomas Wells Dickinson, was an attorney and partner with the largest law firm in New Haven and the issue of the Stanhope J. Dickinsons, a pair of bluenoses from the neighboring town of Simsbury. They claimed lineage dating to the Mayflower but couldn't get confirmation further back than the Revolution. Boasting DAR membership though, seemed eminently satisfying to them.

Their other son, Stanhope Junior, was two years older than Tom, and the area's most well-known and richest antique dealer. A confirmed bachelor, he had a well-earned reputation as a roué and raconteur and lived in one of the fine old colonial homes fronting on Main Street, Farmington. He was seven years older than Mike, and on the surface seemed to everyone to be a genuinely nice guy.

"Well, I guess that's what we do then," Mike said to himself. "Mary can't say no; she's my sis. And the girls will love having Jimmy around. I'll have Jimmy on the phone with me, and we'll ask her together; she'll have to agree."

Surprised at himself that this solution hadn't presented itself earlier, Mike whistled softly on his way through the kitchen to Jimmy's room. "Yes!" he exclaimed, as he pulled a beer out of the fridge and flicked the twist cap toward the trash. "Yes! Everyone is going to love this."

Jimmy was already up and sitting on the rug in his room with his castle blocks strewn about him and what looked like a nearly square heap topped off with crenellated stonework. "Daddy, look at my castle. It's impregal, like you showed me."

"Good for you, Jimmy. That's a big word, but it's im-preg-nable. Try it again."

A perfect mime since he first learned to say Dada, Jimmy looked right at Mike and precisely repeated impregnable.

"You're a clever lad," Mike said. "What's it mean?"

"No one will ever be able to get in my castle," said Jimmy. "Just like what Mommy said about you and me. Nobody but you and me would ever get into her heart. Right, Daddy?"

The lump and the choke came fast that time. *God*, he thought, *Why do I keep getting blindsided like this?* He leaned back to take a long pull on his beer and splutter a bit and wipe his eyes. *Get control.* Softly then, "Right, Jimmy—Mommy's heart. But Mommy let everybody who asked come into her heart. You know that."

For a moment, Jimmy just sat quietly. Then he said, "Not Aunt Mary, Daddy. Mommy said Aunt Mary didn't like her because Mommy was 'Talian.'"

"Mommy said that?" Marie had never said anything like that to Mike.

"Mommy said Aunt Mary was bad, and she didn't trust her. And to only let people you trust into your heart. Why Daddy?"

"I don't know, Jimmy. I'm not sure what Mommy meant. You like Aunt Mary, don't you?"

"I guess so, but what about..."

"Don't worry about that, Jimmy. Mommy must have meant something else. I wanted to ask Aunt Mary if she would take care of you."

"No, Daddy. No." Jimmy started to cry, and Mike held him closely until he stopped. It wasn't a long cry, but it seemed to be, and it troubled Mike.

CHAPTER THREE

Hours later, after Mike and Jimmy, together, calmed down, had supper, said prayers, and Jimmy had gone to bed, Mike sat staring at the family photo taken last Christmas at Martha and Stanhope Dickinson's Simsbury home. Marie's cancer had metastasized by then; a dangerous but apparently easy-to-deal-with melanoma had gone ballistic—inside left wrist (excised and skin grafted) to left armpit lymph nodes, to liver, lungs, and brain—an appalling, disgusting attack, which no amount of chemo or radiation treatment could beat back.

But look at her, he thought. *Just as cheerful and expressive as ever. A bit drawn, but what the hell—we all were sure she'd be done with that crap in a few weeks. "Just one more visit," we all kept saying. "Next month, and we'll all be okay. Marie's a winne*r!"

As he sat there with the photograph in his lap, Mike could see that no one was as absurdly cheerful as he and Marie were trying to be. The tense, frozen grins, hard eyes, stiff expressions and postures—except for the younger children—were now all too obvious. Even among his parents, visiting from Wellesley, and the elder Dickinsons. And he suddenly realized that there really wasn't much sorrow or heartfelt concern there.

He was seeing expressions of boredom, disdain, discomfort. His sister Mary's eyes were sort of rolled back like she was staring at the ceiling in a kind of, "Can we please get done with this?" expression.

Mary's brother-in-law's eyes were deflected to the left, toward Marie, and he was wearing that smug expression he put on whenever he was around Marie. This was Stan Dickinson, and Mike had asked Marie about that after they had been married and learned from her that Stan had propositioned her at the engagement party. Mike was outraged, and Marie defused the revelation by reminding him Stan was drunk and that was probably the cause of his bad behavior. Mike was doubtful but let it go; now noticing for the first time Stan's leer in the photo, Mike's anger re-surfaced, and he wished he'd warned Stan off years ago.

Looking back at Mary's stiff, selfish expression in the photo he thought, *Well screw you. Here it is, Christmas. And Marie is dying. And all you're thinking about is, "Let's open the gifts, have dinner, get rid of my dumb Irish brother and his sick, 'Talian' wife, and finally enjoy Christmas with people who have an appreciation of position, worth, and self-respect." Screw you,* he said again to himself. *Screw all of you sanctimonious shitheads.* Mike raised the framed photograph to smash it against the tabletop and stopped with a shudder. "What the hell am I doing? What's this? I'm going to cut myself and bleed to death? For Christ's sake, Mike." He put the frame back on the table and picked up his beer instead. "Yeah, what the hell. Who wants Jimmy mixed up with them? Screw 'em all."

It was hard for Mike to come to grips with all that had happened this day—the Torellis' flat reversal of their promises, the shock of Jimmy's revelation of his mother's feelings about his sister (which she had shared with Jimmy but not with him), and now the apparent corroboration in the photograph. It was impossible to even think about calling Mary. Not for help. But what about next week? You have to call sometime. Someone's going to call at the next birthday. Even phonies have to pretend they're not. Who ever wants to be the one who starts trouble in a family? What does he do anyway? Call up and say, "Hey, Mary, I know you don't think much about me, and Jimmy tells me you don't like 'Talians.'" Or, "I can see it right in the Christmas picture. You never liked Marie at all." How do you do that?

Does he call his folks and, like some psychotic, say he thinks his sister's family is down on him—and has been? It occurred to him that maybe that was precisely why Marie had not told him what she was aware of and how she felt about it. *What a family fight that would have been,* he thought. Would he have taken her seriously?

So that's it. Say nothing, and just slide into those black crevasses that swallow up families and friends because no one dares to confront the unbelievable and unspeakable conflicts that disrupt and corrupt families.

"Oh hell, Marie," Mike said out loud. "Why would you tell Jimmy something like that—that the Dickinsons are bad people and don't like Italians? Who started that? Not you I hope. Your folks? Maybe Mary was just as scared as we were at Christmas. Goddamnit."

It was going on eight o'clock, and if Mike knew a baby-sitter nearby he would have called him or her over and gone to Phelan's. But he didn't, so he went into the kitchen for another beer, deciding he could drink just as well at home. Besides, he still had some hard thinking to do.

* * * * *

When Marie was scaring everyone to death because of her unexpected relapse, which, despite her calm, quiet courage had tossed Mike into a panic, the possibility of her dying came up. One Saturday morning she was seated at the kitchen table with Mike standing behind her combing her lovely thick hair and massaging the back of her head and neck. This was a weekend ritual for them, and Marie luxuriated in it; missing it later on was probably one of the worst side effects of the radiation therapy.

Now, with her back to Mike she said, "What do you think about daycare centers?"

Mike was momentarily confused by this unexpected subject but caught up quickly. "We're not going to talk about that, honey. We'll only need that if we're going to be off for a wedding in Maine and can't get a baby-sitter. Come on."

"No, Mike," she persisted, "it's just as okay to talk about this now as anytime. Suppose I got hit by a car crossing the street? I'll feel better knowing that we agree about who takes care of Jimmy."

"Okay. Suppose *I* get hit by a car crossing the street," Mike said. "*Then* who's going to take care of Jimmy? And you?"

Mike felt the involuntary tremor that arched up her spine and realized why she'd chosen this moment to talk about care. She knew she would cry and didn't want Mike to see her, but he could feel her pain, and he stepped around the chair to face her. Marie lowered her head and brought her hands up to her eyes, but Mike took both of them in his, put them on his own face, and kissed her long and lovingly on the lips. Then his arms went around her, and he pulled her to him and just held her until the soundless sobbing ceased.

"You're a tough lady you know." Mike couldn't believe how tough she was to be willing to take on a subject like this one. "I guess you're right, Marie. I know you are. And thank God, too; I'd never be able to bring it up."

So they talked about daycare centers and baby-sitters and live-in nannies ("Not on your life," threatened Marie, and they both laughed.) And they speculated about help from in-laws. From what they had heard and seen about daycare centers, there were plenty of advantages, but the risks were enormous. Basic care was one thing, but attention and appreciation and interaction with other children were another. And what about love? Forget about all the stories about abuse.

Marie raised the question herself a week or two later at Sunday dinner with her folks in East Haven. "Oh for God's sake, Marie. What makes you talk like that?" Her mother was on the edge of complete loss of control while Thomas fiddled with the wedge of Parmesan cheese and the cheese grater. It was difficult for all of them having to force their concentration on the likelihood, now perhaps inevitability, of Marie dying; but with her recognizing that possibility far better than they,

they were able to at least deal with it despite the down-deep anguish that screamed within each of them.

As anyone would have expected—given even lesser circumstances—both Fran and Thomas pledged their absolute devotion to Jimmy and Mike. And they pledged themselves to providing whatever help would be needed. "Don't even think about it, Marie," Fran told her daughter. "It will never come to this. But while you're getting better, just stop thinking about, *What's going to happen...?* Right, baby?" Even when her mother was decidedly not in charge, she assumed absolute control. And guess what? Life went on; just look at her brow-beaten husband, Thomas.

This committal was a relief, and Marie agreed with Mike to end further speculation about daycare centers. No one else in their extended families ever raised the issue, so it was set aside. But Mike was sure that, like a tumor, the issue was subconsciously active. Who, for example, ever walks up to the patient and says, "Hey, you'd never know you had cancer. You look great. Does it hurt anywhere?"

At work though, Mike paid increasingly more attention to office talk (praise and complaints) about the rigor, benefits, necessity and, of course, salvation provided by these cute, expensive, and sometimes nasty places that took the place of parents of young children while the parents were at work.

For the most part the need for care was a part of the dues paid by a marriage that needed two incomes, and this distressed Mike. He thought about the impact on the child and figured it was up to the parents if their child grew older a bit screwed up because they needed extra money for a boat or a bigger house or a vacation cruise—whatever. It pained him trying to bring into perspective the widow—or widower—who didn't have an alternative.

So Mike became conversant with the logical and conditionally reasonable alternatives if family, in-laws, nannies, whoever, weren't available—or possible. He was also acutely aware of the mothers at Channel 5 (no fathers, as far as he knew—and he knew) whose daycare child created all sorts of challenges for the parent. The easy stuff was recurring red eye, head lice, colds, and other contagion that obligated the parent to remove "the patient" for the appropriate period. Not so easy, of course, was engaging the terribly expensive sitter who would care for the child for the duration. And unspeakable were the workplace repercussions when the parent was forced to stay home from the job, nursing his or her child back to a condition of re-admissibility to "The Roost," or whatever their care facility was called.

The worst, Mike realized, were the situations of real psychological trauma—some caused by abuse, but most (insidiously and often un-read by both parents and daycare administrators and staff) were those caused by lack of deep caring, attention, and love.

Day after day Mike listened to or overheard disturbing stories about children who couldn't get to sleep or awoke repeatedly during the night or wet their beds (at five years old) or cried if a door slammed or refused to kiss their fathers goodnight or goodbye—or hello for that matter. *Unbelievable,* he thought, *and unbearable to a conscious parent.*

Still at the kitchen table, Mike looked down to see three empties were lined up like the soldiers they used to be. "Well, well, well," he grinned. Then he giggled, and that became the belly laugh you encounter in gin mills, where honest working stiffs hang out, where they're willing to respond with an honest guffaw—not the polite, sissy titters you hear in those joints with the fuzzy wallpaper and the country club manners. He erupted at that with his own guffaw and accidentally swung two bottles onto the floor. "Ah, Mike. You've had it now," he said. "What would Marie be telling you now, you dumb Mick?"

He swept up the mess, scrawled a note on the pad by the phone, and left the pad in the middle of the table. It read: "Jimmy to work."

Then Mike fell into his bed—fully clothed—and the beer swept him into sleep before the wracking dreams took hold.

CHAPTER FOUR

The dreams eventually broke through the alcohol barrier that clouded his thinking mechanisms and induced the familiar, though always unwelcome, resonance of brain outrage. Not the pain and the awful and enduring hangovers of youth though, just a somber, take-charge and pervasive statement punctuating the previous day's behavior. Like a body builder whose muscles always remind him or her of the rigors of the prior day's workout, so too do the body and brain of a drinker like Mike hoarsely whisper for relief.

And Mike whispered back, "What time is it, and why is that TV so loud?" Then, much louder, "Jimmy, what are you doing out there?"

The answer came in Jimmy's controlled and loving voice two or three inches from Mike's ear. "I couldn't get the alarm to work, Daddy, so I used the television. That always gets you up on weekends." Jimmy showed a grin that reminded Mike so much of Marie he could have cried. Instead, he swung his arm over the side of the bed and pulled Jimmy off his feet right into the midst of the covers and down into "tickle-land." "Daddy, Daddy, Daddy, nooooo. Ahhh!" Jimmy shrieked with delight and the helplessness that always comes when a superior force is tickling you into downright loss of control and submission.

"What, what, what?" asked Mike as he rolled over and Jimmy popped out on the other side.

Jimmy squealed, "Peepee, Daddy. Peepee!" and Mike instantly released him and pointed him at the doorway and to the bathroom halfway down the hall.

At breakfast, Mike explained to his son that he would be his important helper at work that day, and he expected his best behavior. "And that includes taking a nap on the couch in my office after lunch, young man," Mike said.

Channel 5 was one of the dominant television stations between New York and Boston, with a viewing audience extending from the Stamford, Connecticut area to the west, right up into Providence, Rhode Island to the east. Significant numbers of viewers also came from the south across Long Island Sound into eastern Long Island, New York. Hartford stations to the north prevented Channel 5 from monopolizing the so-called Hartford/New Haven Area of Dominant Influence (ADI).

It was Mike's job to sell advertising time to the local—generally retail—businesses within that ADI. And, like all the other dozen or so local sales people, he had built his own (now substantial) list of customer accounts over the twelve years he had been with the station.

Unlike newspaper, radio or outdoor advertising, television had always been capable of delivering larger audiences and, therefore, commanding higher prices for its advertising time. The industry's higher revenues generally attracted smarter, better educated, and more aggressive sales people. And the medium itself, with television programming coming over the network feed from New York, Los Angeles, or around the world, simply made broadcast television a more glamorous business to be in.

Mike had learned all about this as a summer intern at a small ad agency in Worcester, Massachusetts. Despite his father's desperate pleas to follow in his footsteps by matriculating at Boston College, Mike had applied to only Notre Dame and Holy Cross. As he expected, ND didn't want him and "The Cross" did, so he spent four years at BC's arch-rival and annually, with his dad, made the ritual bet on the outcome of the BC-Holy Cross game.

He did take his father's advice about a possible career path however, and that helped decide his college major. Over the years, it had become obvious to his father that the fun, the expense accounts, the trips, free tickets, and commission income went to the people who sold advertising space at the *Boston Herald*. Reporters like he seldom got perks beyond an automobile, and even that couldn't be driven for personal use.

So at Holy Cross Mike signed up for Marketing Communications with a minor in Advertising, learned about "media," and got first-hand experience at his summer job at the ad agency. Like all interns and most new hires in fact, the grunt work was found in the media department, and that's where Mike spent the summer between his sophomore and junior years.

During his senior year he made a pest of himself, telephoning the various television salespeople who during the summer had called on him at the ad agency. His persistence paid off—not in a sales job, which would be far too much of a plum for a newbie—but Worcester's WORC-TV, Channel 4, hired him as a "gofer" in their traffic department.

When Mike had been at the ad agency he had developed through hearsay and innuendo a sort of disdain for the nerds (generally) who performed trafficking functions at the TV, cable, and radio stations. Within days of joining WORC-TV, however, his grandfather's political skills for parlaying opportunity into influence emerged in Mike, and he realized that it was in trafficking where the real power resided at a television station.

What he discovered was that, despite all the promises and protestations a salesperson might make— either to their media buyer (at an agency) or to the actual client (at the car dealership, for example)— it was the lowly traffic manager who decided at exactly what time a commercial would be scheduled for broadcast.

What sort of power did this represent? If a particular client flipped on WORC-TV between six-thirty and seven-thirty in the morning, expected to see their commercial, and the salesperson had promised—as part of the deal—that they *would* see it, it was the traffic manager's responsibility to write the schedule so that the broadcast engineers ran it at that time.

The traffic manager had a lot of latitude. Let's say the commercial was scheduled for seven twenty-nine, and the client, impatient, stomped out of their kitchen at seven twenty-eight and missed it. Who caught the heat? The salesperson. This was significant leverage and was greased with flowers, lunches, cute little "Have A Nice Day" cards, tickets to sporting events, shows and concerts, discounts at local merchants, free dinners at area restaurants; there was no end to the power that could be claimed by the "nerd back in traffic."

Was it an apparently natural attribute of Mike's to recognize and exploit this leverage? Of course! Did he? He was so good at it that the sales staff (only four people at the time) was desperate to get him moved out of traffic and into sales so the overworked, stressed, but malleable and dependable, former traffic "nerd" could resume his compliant and clueless responsibilities.

So that's how Mike Flynn got started, and in less than five years the larger, richer ABC Network affiliate in New Haven had learned about his talent and offered him the same job but with bigger accounts, a larger office, a newer car, and the opportunity to make much more money. At seven-thirty that morning he and Jimmy were headed for the station.

No one had yet arrived in the administrative and sales offices when the Flynns walked through the back door ten minutes later. But the station had been on the air for nearly three hours, and Studio One was abuzz with activity. The anchors for the local morning news and the weather team had been broadcasting live since six o'clock, which meant the entire production, news, and support staffs were there as well.

Some staff members were long-used to the "show biz" part of television, but not Mike. He always felt he was backstage at some big

Broadway production or Radio City Music Hall or the circus. He loved this part of the business, and he infected his clients and prospects with the same enthusiasm by sharing the "backstage" experiences with them.

Several years before, he had convinced station management to construct a soundproof booth right in the main studio where visitors could sit and watch live newscasts and weather and the local, mid-morning and late afternoon talk shows that Channel 5 produced. Inside, the booth was strictly *Hollywood*, with comfortable lounge chairs, a richly upholstered sofa, phones, an oversized monitor, and call buttons to order in coffee, soft drinks, and other refreshments. Guests loved it when Dr. Bob, the weatherman, dropped in between his on-air forecasts to chitchat while he refilled his coffee cup. "Oh my God, it's Dr. Bob," they would exclaim. "Dr. Bob, I watch you all the time," they would prate unconvincingly. "Oh, Dr. Bob, will you autograph this please? It's for my husband" (or wife, or niece...never for them)." No matter. The booth was special, and it helped to add millions, over the years, to the station's revenues.

Mike and Jimmy stopped in the kitchen on their way to Mike's office to get apple juice for Jimmy, coffee for Mike, and the *New Haven Register* to catch up on events over the weekend. Jimmy made himself comfortable in one of Mike's swivel armchairs to watch the ever-present monitor, but he quickly became impatient with the news and asked for some kids' entertainment. Unfortunately, it was considered taboo to tune to any station other than Channel 5 in order to keep an eye on the rotation and proper broadcast of your clients' commercials. Mike usually spent at least an hour every evening however, watching the other stations, including cable systems, to discover any new advertisers that might have bought time with his competition.

Fortunately, Jimmy had brought his Game Boy, and he booted that up, stretched out on the couch, and quickly became absorbed in the tiny, mesmerizing game figures on the screen.

As the time wound on to nine o'clock, the buzz of conversation rose, and the tempo of, "Good morning, Mikes," increased. When one or two staffers poked their heads far enough into the office to spot Jimmy, there was a brief explanation and a, "Have fun, Jimmy," in response. Things were going well, Jimmy was comfortable, and Mike was happy to be back at work.

Dave Batchelder, vice president of sales, held a meeting every Monday at ten o'clock to review month-to-date sales performance, learn what plans were for the coming week, configure pricing strategies, and announce special programming that would be coming from the network.

On his way out of the meeting, Dave motioned for Mike to stay behind. "How's it going with you two?" he asked Mike. "He's a nice looking boy. Sure can see Marie, huh?"

"Yup. Big eyes. Big grin. We're doing fine. Adjusting. We'll be all right." Mike knew he didn't sound that convincing.

"So what are your plans for Jimmy? Didn't you tell me your in-laws were going to take care of him? They're local, right?"

"That's what the deal was," Mike said. "Yeah, they live in East Haven, but something's come up. Yesterday they told me they can't watch him, so I've got to work something out."

"When will you do that?" asked Dave.

"What the hell kind of question is that?" Mike said. "I'd expect you to say can I help you out or have you thought about, whatever. For Christ's sake, Dave." Mike was still reeling from yesterday's unexpected news from his in-laws and surprised even himself with his sharp retort.

"Hey, hey, hey. Settle down, Mike. I'm just asking."

"Fine, a couple days. What's the difference? My list is under control."

"Mike, you're doing fine. You've always done fine. Nancy asked me to talk to you." Well into her fifties, Nancy had worked her way from out behind the reception desk years ago to first handle payroll, then vacations and sick days, and finally became the Personnel Manager. She was mean-spirited and just loved pushing people to the edge. With the new practice of calling these types Human Resource Managers, Nancy tended to go over the edge as often as she thought she could get away with it. Few at the station liked her, and Mike wouldn't let her get away with anything.

"Talk to me?" Mike's voice produced the hard edge that he mostly saved for trouble. "What does she want you to talk to me about? We got a problem with Jimmy, here?" Mike's defenses began going up fast. "It's not even lunchtime on a Monday morning, everyone in the place is late to work, and you're telling me Nancy's got a problem with my kid? What's her goddamn problem?"

"Mike, it's not her problem. Channel 5 doesn't have liability coverage for kids in the station. So it's the station's problem, and she's telling us because it's her job." Dave was trying to maintain some perspective, but Mike wasn't buying it.

"Kids in the station? What about the school groups that come through? What about the cutesy little models? What about the sound room in Studio One? Kids are allowed in there. Want me to make Jimmy sit in there all day?"

"Mike," Dave started, but Mike cut him off.

"The hell with it Dave. This is bullshit, and you know it. And you ought to know better than to put up with her crap. But we'll help you out by not putting up with yours. We're leaving."

CHAPTER FIVE

Ten minutes later, Mike was at the bar in Phelan's telling Tim Halloran what had happened at the station, and Tim was dutifully nodding his head in sympathy. Jimmy was in a booth with a cherry coke, and Heather was fixing him a sandwich. Mike was draining his Elm City draught, and another was on its way. "Can you believe it, Tim? Thank God *you* let kids in."

"Well they're really only allowed in the booths you know, not at the bar. And an adult is supposed to be sitting in the booth with them. But I'm not one for tossing out kids. When they're here there's an important reason. You gotta go with the flow."

Phelan's lunch crowd was a mixture of white-collar and blue-collar men and women. White, tan, and black, most of them were familiar, if not known, to each other, and all of them valued the place for its fairly priced and delicious sandwiches and soups. Most also had a drink; not many had two. The ones that did, like Mike, could handle it, and no one commented if they got a little loud—or a little quiet. As the number of today's patrons grew, Mike picked up his third beer from the bar and moved into the booth with his son.

On the drive from the station, Mike had explained to Jimmy what had happened—that it was just a company rule—couldn't stay all day, okay to visit for a while. And when he reminded Jimmy about their earlier conversations about daycare, he was happy to see him brighten up. Jimmy had been neutral the first time they talked about it but more interested than not. Now he seemed to be looking forward to giving it a try.

"What kind of sandwich did Heather fix for you?" Mike asked. It was gone but for a piece of crust and a few chips.

"She said it was ham salad, but it tasted like tuna fish. That's okay. I like tuna fish. The pickle was better than at home."

"Well I'm glad to know you liked the pickle, young man."

Heather was laughing as she came from behind the row of booths. "So you like tuna fish. I'm glad, because I gave you the wrong sandwich. Your ham salad went to the lady over there. Problem is she loves tuna and hates ham, so yours is back in the kitchen. Sorry, Jimmy." They both laughed together.

"I'll have his/her ham salad," said Mike. "What kind of bread is that one on?"

"You'll get a fresh one, Mike. You like rye, right? And no baloney today?" Heather winked and moved on as Mike grinned back and shook his head.

Mike had been worried about taking the next steps in getting care for Jimmy, but the beer had loosened him up and he felt braver about calling a pre-Marie friend from the station who had offered help well before his wife had died.

"Jimmy, I've got to call the station. Just try not to eat my sandwich when Heather brings it okay?" He reached out and pulled on Jimmy's closest ear, and then pulled Jimmy as close as he could, across the table. When Jimmy said, "Ouch," Mike said, "I love you, Jimmy." And then he tweaked the other ear.

Meg Donlon, the traffic manager at Channel 5, had joined the station in July, 1985 as an "editorial assistant" in the newsroom. At that time, her mother, Maureen, was the station's frontline receptionist where she had reigned since 1968. "Mo," as she was known by staffers and clients alike, was thirty-one years old when she was hired, and her wonderful, spontaneous sense of humor, enviable class, refined good looks, and correct sense of grooming exemplified the personality and style the station worked hard to promote. There was no question about whether or not a suitable position could be found for her daughter, who was baptized Mary Margaret. This was shortened to Meg during her college years at Albertus Magnus College, a women's school in New Haven, owned and run by the Dominican nuns.

Mike Flynn had been at Channel 5 since June, 1983, just two years before Meg came on board, and at twenty-eight years old he was six years her senior. As a Holy Cross grad, he was of the religious persuasion that Meg's Roman Catholic father, Frank (Francis Xavier) Donlon, could embrace. As the mentor who stepped up to help her acclimate to the television business, she had been bowled over. And as the husky, handsome, thick-haired Irishman that he was, she fell in love with Mike at once.

Unfortunately for Meg, soon after Mike had joined Channel 5 he had quickly become known as an eligible bachelor as well as a social butterfly. He was popular throughout New Haven and the Yale community and was invited to more functions than he could attend. Not only that, Channel 5 events such as on-site promotions at shopping centers and major retail outlets and functions like United Way fund-raisers, made him easily visible to a broad spectrum of the community.

So Mike had a solid social calendar, and he made sure Meg was invited to most functions to help her broaden her own social network. And, of course, he'd known her mother, Mo, for a couple of earlier years and had seen Meg visiting the station. So it seemed to him more of a "family" relationship, and at first he deliberately maintained a strictly friends-only basis.

But over time, Mike was drawn more and more to Meg, and for a while they engaged in a steamy relationship that carried on for several months but suddenly came to an end just before it was consummated.

For a while, Meg simply pined for Mike as any young adult but distant admirer would. But as the months passed, Mo had to counsel her on the range of Mike's activities and distractions—and likely attractions. For weeks Meg was desolate and completely in the dark as to the cause of this, until word got out that Mike was seeing someone else.

Overnight she grew up fast and learned an abrupt lesson in the game of romance. And it was hard for her. After a while she stopped feeling sorry for herself; stopped crying herself to sleep at night; and stopped catching her breath hoping for Mike to tire of his new attraction.

As it happened—as Meg mournfully realized it was bound to happen—the news of Mike's Christmas 1987 engagement was known by everyone at Channel 5 within minutes of the beginning of the first working day after the Christmas/New Year's holiday break. Mo, of course, had heard it first, and the first thing a loving mother would do, and she did, was to call Meg, who answered the phone, "Happy New Year, this is Meg in Traffic."

"Happy New Year to you, sweetie, even though I think I've given you a dozen of them and maybe two dozen eggnogs to go with them." Then, testing the air, Mo asked, "What's up?"

"Why are you asking me, Mom? You know nothing happens on a Tuesday after a holiday. Come on, *you* told *me* that! What's up with you? You want to have coffee together?"

"Yup! Why don't you get some for both of us from the kitchen and hop out here to reception. Glad to know you're not doing a thing." Mo's chuckle was cut off by an incoming call and her, "Happy New Year. How may Channel 5 help you today?"

* * * * *

Mo had just finished with the news about Mike and was at first surprised and then relieved that Meg was not only miles from the silent sufferer she had expected but was stoically nodding her acceptance of the news.

"Happy New Year, Mo, Meg. Hey, it's good to see you two." Mike Flynn's breath was steaming as he stood in front of the safety-glassed reception area with his dark, wide-set eyes and huge Irish grin. He stuck his arm over the top of the safety partition and lowered a bottle of a dramatically inexpensive, but not too bad, split of faux champagne with a red ribbon knotted in a bow and tied round its diminutive neck.

Meg jumped in fast before her mother could initiate a protective response in her behalf. "Mike! We've just heard the great news; happy New Year to you! And congratulations. Who's the lucky girl?" Mo was so proud of Meg that tiny tears squeezed out of the corners of her eyes.

Touched by Mo's tears, Mike was also aglow with pleasure at Meg's good wishes, and Mo instantly echoed her daughter's sentiments with, "God bless you, Mike. Tell us. Who is it?"

The next few minutes were consumed with Mike's response about a Marie someone from East Haven, and with their oohs and ahhs and repeated good wishes and Mike exultant and Meg beginning to shake with self-pity. And with Mo trembling with angst for her daughter and bursting with pride for Meg's solid and beautifully mature response to Mike's killer-confirmation of the earlier news.

Then Mike blew kisses through the security barrier to both of them and left the reception area for his office. Mo turned to look at her daughter, whose eyes were still fixed on the doorway Mike had taken. "It's time to let him go isn't it, Meg?" she said.

"Of course it is, Mom. I figured this would happen long ago, but don't you just love watching the way he moves?"

Big sigh of relief (and pride, happiness, and all the other stuff that doting mothers are supposed to, and *do*, feel) from Mo, then, "Well, what are we waiting for, Meg? Let's have some Champers!"

Since a time buyer from the London ad agency which handled Land Rover had visited a couple years ago with a case of Champagne and urging, "Champers for all," Mo had referred to bubbly (of any origin, French or otherwise) as "Champers."

Meanwhile, Mo had to agree that she loved to watch the way Mike moved, but she'd never admit that to her daughter. No way!

That was seven years ago, and now Mike's bride was dead and he was calling Meg from Phelan's bar.

Meg answered her direct line with, "Hi, this is Meg in Traffic, how may I help you?"

Mike assumed the disguise he used years ago when Meg was new to the business world, new to the station, and new to the sometime antics he used on novices like her. These generally included slightly lascivious remarks which, coming from anyone other than the charming and altogether too innocent Mike Flynn, would probably embarrass or offend most people. Mike could always carry it off, though, simply because they really knew it was all a joke. And he *was* funny.

One of his routines involved a low, muffled voice with an obvious Bronx accent and heavy, pulsing breathing. So when Meg put her phone to her ear Mike growled out, "Yes, is this the traffic department?" Meg knew in an instant it was Mike and picked up the routine saying, "This is the Channel 5 traffic department, how may I help you?" Mike said, "I've just run three red lights, I've been speeding down Orange Street, my registration has expired and I'm naked; I need a lot of help from the Traffic Department. What can you do for me?"

Usually Meg (and most of the others Mike kidded with) would say, "Oh for God's sake, Mike, will you cut that out? You are a grown-up." But today she said, "*You* have been very naughty. I'm going to have to ask you to step in here for a spanking. *You* are a bad, bad boy."

"Hey, Meg! It's me, Mike," he blurted into the phone. "What is the matter with you? Do you get calls like this all the time? What's up with you?"

Meg said, "Mike who? Exactly who is this traffic violator? I'm going to report you to Nancy in Personnel. She'll know how to deal with a pervert like you!"

"Meg! Wait, Meg, it's me, Mike. Come on, Meg it's me!"

"Excuse me? I'm not sure I know a Mike with a voice like that. Would that be my old boyfriend, Mike Kelly? Or would that be Nancy's perverted, sadistic lover, Mike Flynn?" Meg said.

"Mary Margaret, you are a slug. I would ordinarily hang up this phone this instant but I called collect, and I'm not paying for the call. How can you be so ridiculous?"

"Oh my God, is this you Mike? Mike Flynn! Jesus, Mary and Joseph, I can't believe what I'm hearing." Meg was adopting the brogue she had heard from her father all throughout her childhood. "I know the little people run naked through the woods and put shamrocks in their hair but you, John Michael Flynn, a grown man, driving naked through red lights in downtown New Haven. Well, I just don't know about people like you. How long has this been going on anyway?"

Meg had won this one, and Mike gave her full credit. "You got me, Meg," he said. "And with the cute reference to Nancy, I guess you've heard what happened to Jimmy and me this morning. I'm glad I called; you're making me feel better already."

"Mike, I hear about nearly every step you take. I probably shouldn't tell you that, but it's true. So there. Meanwhile, what are you doing with Jimmy?"

"That's why I called, Meg. It's not going to work out with either my family or my in-laws, so I'm thinking about daycare, and since the traffic manager knows everything about all that matters in life, I figured you could point Jimmy and me in the right direction."

"You mean 'who's who' and 'what's what' in quality, local daycare?" Meg's first reaction was to feel disappointed about the motivation of his call, but she was more mature now, and actually appreciated that he valued her for at least her viewpoint, if not actual advice. Then, "Actually, Mike, I called Mom just after I heard about Dave's insensitive...well, what the hell does he know about manners and tact?"

"Yeah. But he's probably right. Damn thing is that bitch Nancy acting like she owns the world and can just jump on people whenever she feels like it. *She's* the sadist. What did Mo say?"

"She said to ask you and Jimmy for dinner tonight at her place, and we could all talk about it together. I'm invited too, so you can't say no. Be there at six o'clock. And one other thing—don't be naked!"

CHAPTER SIX

After his call to Meg, Mike enjoyed his chips, pickle, and sandwich and some beery small talk with Jimmy, then called the sales department to let them know he would be back in the office the next morning. The group secretary (and the only one with any business sense and discipline, and without whom the sales group would cease to function), Michelle Laker, quietly asked if everything was alright.

"Thanks, Michelle," Mike said. "Things could certainly be a lot worse, but Jimmy and I are okay, and with pals like you we'll be better than ever. Anyway, I won't be in as early tomorrow, but I should be there close to nine. Any calls?"

"Well, Dave was asking for you, but we're covering, and he'll probably realize by tomorrow that he was way out of line—if we're lucky."

"If *he's* lucky and his cranial circuit breaker clicks on," Mike said. "Thanks, Michelle."

* * * * *

"Guess what?" Mike said during the short drive from Phelan's to their apartment, and Jimmy said, "When we get home we're both going to take naps. And then you'll drink some beer and I'll watch TV. After you call your friends, we'll either have franks with baked beans or spaghetti with Ragu meat sauce. If we have spaghetti I want some garlic bread like Mommy used to make. Okay?"

Mike flushed red with Jimmy's precise and all too frank summation of the sort of parent he'd been over the past several weeks. Jimmy certainly wasn't condemnatory, but his innocent and candid recitation of Mike's beer, phone calls, and franks-and-beans routine startled Mike with its clarity and honesty. He admitted he had to do a lot better, but he wondered if he could.

"Jimmy, you're right. We're both taking naps. But then we'll have a hot shower, put on our nice clothes, get some flowers down at the corner, and drive over to Aunt Mo's. Do you remember her?"

Squealing with delight, Jimmy said, "The Toll House Cookie lady. Right, Daddy?"

"And what else?" Mike asked. He wasn't surprised that Jimmy would make the cookie connection.

"She's the nice lady who used to work at the station, and her sister Meg works there, right?"

"That will make Aunt Mo feel very special if you say that to her, Jimmy, but Meg is Aunt Mo's daughter, not her sister. And she'll be there tonight too."

"Meg is *so* nice. When Mommy was sick in the hospital and you brought me to the office to meet that other baby-sitter I didn't like, Meg read stories to me. Do you know she's a good reader?"

"I didn't know that, Jimmy. But I think she can also make up good stories. When you see her, ask if she'll tell you a story about the 'little people.' And ask her if she'll do it in an Irish accent."

"An irishcent? What's that, Daddy?"

"Jimmy, you and I are descended from people across the Atlantic Ocean in Ireland, where they used to speak a different language. And when they came here and learned to speak American they still had an accent, which sounded like the language they used to speak. So it's 'accent'—an Irish accent; two words."

"But why would Meg tell me a story with an Irish cent? Why not her regular cent?"

"Okay, Jimmy, that's a very clever question. And as you know, you are a very clever boy. So, first of all it is ac-cent—not cent. But don't worry about that. Secondly, lots of times when people tell stories about Irish people or Italian people or Jewish people—it's mainly those people—when they use an accent it makes the story more believable. And most of the time it's funnier!"

Jimmy said, "Daddy, you know when you tell those stories over at Phelan's and sometimes I can't understand you, and everybody is laughing and singing and slapping your back? Is that Irish?"

"Good for you, Jimmy! That's exactly what I mean. And if you really *are* Italian or Jewish or Irish, the story is *a lot* funnier. Someday we'll call your granduncle, my mother's cousin, Tom O'Sullivan. When he tells you a story in his Irish accent you will love it forever!"

"Can he tell a story about the little people too?"

"Of course, but you ask Meg first."

Mo lived in an upscale condominium complex on New Haven's southernmost tip of shoreline overlooking—in fact perched on—New Haven Harbor which emptied into Long Island Sound. Built in 1984, she and Frank, her fifty-three-year-old, and, at the time, still healthy husband, bought a two-bedroom unit at a tremendous traffic-building discount. Their views were to the northeast in the direction of Rhode Island, south across the Sound to Long Island, ten miles away, and west toward New York. The sunrises were splendid and, on the seventh floor, they were out of reach of the foul weather salt spray that so battered the balcony furniture of neighbors on lower floors and begrimed their picture windows nearly year-round.

Meg was in her last year of college then and after graduation had stayed with her parents for a couple years until her increasing Channel 5 earnings permitted her to afford an apartment in New Haven, east of The Green.

The New Haven Green was undoubtedly the model for most New England town greens within three hundred miles. And New England town greens are notorious for preserving, inviolably, the sanctity of their own greensward, whether this is a quarter acre and mostly mud and weeds or an environmental monument to the devotion of the town's settlers. New Haven's Green is a monumental square bordered on the north and east by early, heroic buildings of Yale University, with the east/west axis bisected by the venerable Temple Street, which looms into and terminates in the heart of the Yale campus. It was protected and maintained by a succession of Board Members — trustees who had ensured that it was properly respected and cared for over a period reaching nearly three-hundred years.

So to live and work within a two to three minute walk of New Haven's Green bestowed, generations earlier, much prestige upon the living/working walker. When Dutch elm disease attacked The Green in the 1800s however, the denuded acreage degraded to a muddy, weed-choked barren. This encouraged adjacent (and privileged) landowners, home-owners, and tenants to migrate elsewhere, thus rendering the living spaces equally barren.

While the trustees immediately replanted The Green with Silver Maples, their spindly grandeur took nearly 70 years for townspeople to notice and to embark on a reclamation program of architecturally sound and noteworthy apartments, townhouses, and buildings abutting the city's revitalized symbol of its heritage. These quickly filled with tenants who more or less reflected the near-century earlier hauteur of their ancestors.

In the two and three blocks north and east of The Green however, were houses and tenements which had been homesteaded by folks moving in after the earlier flight of original tenants and had become slums. In the late 1970's though, the city, at the urging of Yale University, encouraged and helped finance a minor renaissance in those neighborhoods, and they had become attractive, chic, and moderately inexpensive places to live. Meg had purchased her third floor, one-bedroom apartment in a narrow but lovely brick townhouse on a block now occupied mostly by young, upscale people like her.

CHAPTER SEVEN

At home, Jimmy happily fell off to sleep while Mike dozed briefly on the living room couch before making calls to a few clients who had become close friends as well. He was pleased no one from the office tried to check up on him, because the last thing he wanted was sympathy out of a sense of duty.

Later, Jimmy came from his nap full of energy and, trotting into the living room, he proudly announced he had even brushed his teeth without being asked. Mike could tell his son was ready to party.

Suddenly Mike said, "Hey, you and I agreed we were really going to get nice for this. We were taking a hot shower! Yowee—into the tub..."

Theirs was a ridiculous routine between them alone, at shower time, featuring a dash down the hallway while pulling off shirts, hopping to kick off shoes, and deliberately tossing their clothing to make a haphazard trail to the bathroom. And so it was now with shrieks and yells and bumping and "Watch its" to win the "Who's Naked First" prize and be into the tub before the other.

Did Mike ever win? Of course not; the entire act evolved from an early ploy to interest Jimmy in regular hygiene by making it fun, to a routine for initiating the locker room antics of boys worldwide. Some dads would call all this "bonding," but Mike absolutely could not understand what "bonding" was all about. "What the hell is this?" he would ask whoever his male drinking partner at Phelan's might be. "Why can't parents understand what simple, basic, parent-to-child love will do? Why can't they understand what simple, basic hugs and simple, basic kisses will do?" While his drinking pal would be cogently nodding, Mike would re-start with, "I mean, for Christ's sake, if you kiss and hug your kids they *know* you *love* them. So when you can't get their attention about something you're *not* happy about, they *still* know you love them even while you might be spanking them."

Once, when his bar-buddy happened to be his sister Mary's lawyer-husband, Tom, what Mike heard drove him from draught beer straight into Scotch whisky. Tom's law firm was only three blocks from Phelan's, nestled up to the New Haven Town Hall at the south end of The Green, and he had called Mike earlier. "I'm not sure Youth and Family Services, let alone the courts, would see it that way," said Tom.

"What are you talking about? So what," asked Mike. "Are you saying that you think a spanking doesn't fit into a parent's prerogatives for upbringing? Is this according to *you* as *well* as to a court of law?"

With obvious disdain, Thomas Wells Dickinson sniffed, "Don't be so naive. You read the papers. Even your own kid can sue you for child abuse. Quite successfully these days, I might add."

They went on that way for the next few minutes, mainly because Mike had arrived at Phelan's before Tom and was two beers up on Tom's single glass of wine. Mike was making a mistake trying to bait this trial lawyer-brother-in-law, and he had become heated and an octave higher than the usual conversational tone of Tim Halloran's bar. During this exchange with Tom speaking loudly, banter had dropped to that of a stage whisper permitting audio voyeurism among the patrons...all but one of them regulars. The "irregular," of course, was Tom picking on their friend, and Mike's pals were standing by to come to his aid if needed. If not, they were hooked on the tone and direction of the conversation, as they would be in response to a prime time television series like "Friends" or "Frasier."

"Okay, Tom. So to you I am incorrect. That's fine. I know that millions of parents around the country would agree with you, and that's something I can't do anything about. Let's pretend you and I didn't get excited about this. Let's talk about what we're doing here. You called me, and I suggested my favorite bar. What's up?"

Tom nodded, took a deep breath, and was about to speak when Mike said, "How about another wine? You ready? Tim, pour me a Scotch this time. Thanks. Tom?"

"This is what Mary and I wanted to talk about, Mike."

"Mary? What does Mary want to talk about? What's wrong? Is everybody okay?"

"Mike." Tom paused—a full stop. "We're all fine, but we wonder if you are. Mary and I are worried about you."

Long pause. "What am I a dope, Tom? Why don't you just say, 'Hey, Mike. How many beers did you put down tonight? You okay, Mike? Hey, Mike. Who's gonna drive you home?'"

"Listen, Mike. We..."

"Don't stiff me, Tom. I'm not some hoity-toity from Farmington for Christ's sake—some fatuous lawyer from a big law firm. Tell me what makes you two so worried."

"Jimmy. That's all," said Tom.

Mike was puzzled. "There's nothing wrong with Jimmy. What do you mean? You said you were worried about me."

Tom took a deep breath and exhaled slowly. He didn't want to show his exasperation, and he never thought he'd have to get this far into it. "Mike, we're worried about what might happen when Jimmy wakes up at night, needs help and you're passed out. And *you* should worry about that, too. You don't have to be a hoity-toity lawyer to figure that out."

"Where is all this coming from? What is this sudden awareness and criticism of my fondness for a few beers?"

"Mike, before Marie got so sick we never cared how many beers you drank—or Scotches for that matter. Marie was always there for both of you. Of *course* we hate to be critical. We're not at all comfortable talking to you about it. But now we're looking beyond just you."

Mike suddenly realized it had become deathly still in the bar. He felt the eyes of his friends on him, and he was embarrassed.

"Okay, Tom. I get the message. Thanks. Tell Mary 'thanks.' You have to go. I'll be leaving soon. Say hi to the girls."

Tom stood to leave and Mike said to him, "Just don't worry. I'll take care of Jimmy."

* * * * *

Mike thought about this confrontation frequently as he was doing now while toweling off with his son. And, while he found it disagreeable that his sister had sent her husband to scold him, he realized they were right about the care he was responsible for providing. So, on the one hand he was surprised to realize he appreciated their concern, while on the other he resented their intrusion.

He also resented Tom's implication that not only did Mike have a problem, but also that they had been aware of the "problem" for some time, perhaps well before Marie was diagnosed. Maybe Marie was aware of it, let it color her opinion, and perhaps fostered her thought that the Dickinsons had problems with the Italians and Irish. Or maybe after too many wines herself, Mary said something snide and hurtful to Marie about her family and about Mike. And maybe Marie didn't want to repeat this to her husband but let it slip out with Jimmy and had no idea how a pre-schooler could hang on to something like that.

"Well?" said Jimmy. "I'm waiting."

"What? Waiting for what?" said Mike.

"Come on, Daddy. You always dry my back."

Mike adopted his "mad scientist" routine saying, "Oh, so the little vun wants to get his back dried up. Okay. Vee do that before vee throw him outside to zee crocodiles."

"No! No, Daddy," shrieked Jimmy. "It's me, and I'm dry!"

"Come here my little vun," growled Mike. And he smothered Jimmy in one of the huge, thick, terrycloth towels Marie had always called her 'luxurious splurge' after paying nearly $40 for the two of them.

Then, before Mike could prolong the agony, Jimmy announced he had to get dressed and comb his hair and to please stop.

Well, thought Mike proudly, *more than a bit of his mother in that one.*

"Okay, Jimmy. I'd like you to put on your nice gray pants and that yellow polo shirt Mommy got for your birthday. I put them on your bed. After I get dressed I'll help you get a straight part in your hair."

Ten minutes later, the two of them were out on the sidewalk where they took a left toward Whitney Avenue. This was the main, south to north thoroughfare in and out of the east side of New Haven, and through some of the most posh neighborhoods in town.

There was a fine multi-national deli on the corner at Whitney, with a splendid array of fresh flowers of all sorts set out on the sidewalk. Patrons were able to select what they wanted and assemble their own arrangements, as well as choose from bouquets already made up. Jimmy knew the routine and immediately began picking out individual stalks of blue and yellow Iris. Mike added a few ferns for texture, and they were ready with a beautiful and abundant armful.

During the five minute drive to Aunt Mo's condominium, Jimmy chattered away looking forward to seeing her and Meg again and anticipating Meg's response when he asked her about the "little people." "Will she really know what they are, Daddy?"

To Jimmy, grown-up people his own size sounded too good to be true, and he was anxious to learn more. Remembering his call to Meg that afternoon, Mike grinned broadly and assured his son that Meg would know. "And," he said, "soon, you'll know, too!"

They parked close to the main entrance in the convenient and thoughtful visitors' spaces and headed through the foyer to the elevators.

"Best behavior, right, Jimmy?"

"Yes, Daddy. You too, right?" Mike blushed beet-red and wondered if Jimmy also thought what Tom and Mary—and who knew who else—thought about him and his fondness for drink.

CHAPTER EIGHT

"Oh I can't believe it," said Mo, exclaiming over the riotous bunch of Irises Jimmy held out to her as she welcomed him through her door. "How beautiful, Jimmy. Come in. Come in, Mike."

"We got them at the deli," said Jimmy. "They're for you and Meg." Then, "Thank you for inviting us."

A sudden, big lump swelled in Mike's throat again. He was so proud of his little gentleman, and he could see Mo was touched as well.

"Well hello," said Meg, coming around the corner from the living room. Mo had taken the flowers from Jimmy, kissing his brow, and Meg stooped to hold Jimmy by the shoulders and give him a welcoming hug. "Look how much you've grown," she said.

Jimmy beamed back at Meg and, unexpectedly, threw his arms around her neck saying, "I missed you."

"And I've missed you, too, Jimmy. The flowers are gorgeous."

Jimmy wasn't the least bit shy in boasting, "I told Daddy you and Aunt Mo would like them," while his dad grinned broadly from a step behind him.

Mo's apartment was on the next to the top floor, and the water views were serene and rich and thoroughly calming. She, Meg, and Mike left Jimmy with a Pepsi in front of the living room television while they went onto the balcony with their cocktails to enjoy the view. Meg was doing the honors for her mother and offered Mike his choice of beverage. "Mom and I are having this white wine, Mike, but I can get you a beer or Scotch or gin." Mike asked for Scotch-on-the-rocks, and the three of them settled into their deck chairs and easy, familiar conversation. It was nearly sunset, and they could just barely feel and enjoy the last of the cooling southwesterly breeze.

After a few minutes of compliments from Mike about her place, and Mo returning them by expressing her pleasure with Jimmy's behavior and obvious adjustment, Meg said, "The station sure isn't giving you much time to develop a plan for Jimmy. What are you going to do?" Sensing these two women were as close to being family as his own, Mike told them about the back-to-back blows he had encountered in just the past two days.

The reversal of the Torellis' earlier assurances of help was as puzzling to Mo and Meg as it had been to Mike. And they were equally puzzled with Mike's report of his sister's dislike of Italians as Jimmy said Marie had told him. What could that be all about? Had Jimmy misunderstood?

Mo had risen, perplexed over the story about Mary, and now returned, still frowning but bearing a fresh Scotch for Mike and pouring wine for Meg and herself.

And then, of course, they all pitched in with speculations about what *possibly* could motivate the station to act so callously. They asked, "Who would Jimmy threaten? "Could Dave really think Mike's sales productivity would slip? "Was there some other message? "Have your numbers slipped all *that* much since the funeral?"

"I don't know what's going on," Mike said. "But I wonder if some of those stiffs are ganging up on me because I turn in so many receipts from Phelan's."

"Well for God's sake," said Meg, "that's legitimate client entertainment, Mike. They all know that."

"Maybe they don't. Maybe someone's thinking I'm belting it back a little too much."

The ladies started polite, supportive protestations but then listened quietly to Mike's story about his confrontation with Tom. "You know I don't like hearing that," Mike said. "But I guess he's entitled to be concerned if he and Mary are right about me. It's tough you know. It's the way I was brought up. Drinking was always part of the family fabric—and the social fabric. Hell, the cultural fabric! And now I'll have another."

They all chuckled, although Mo wasn't as enthusiastic, and she excused herself to put finishing touches to their dinner. As she left, Meg said, "Are you sure you want that Scotch, Mike?" and at his vigorous response, "You bet!" she reluctantly brought him his third.

Because it was easy, and she was good at it, Meg had made lasagna for dinner, and that was now warming, along with a garlic-buttered loaf of Italian bread, in her mother's pre-heated oven. She was tossing some greens with an off-the-shelf dressing and trying to toss out of her head her sudden concerns about Mike's drinking.

On the one hand, she would never have thought much about a guest taking three drinks before dinner. Some people could; some couldn't. On the other hand, Mike seemed, in bringing it up, to be thinking about it—and taking warnings seriously. What did this mean? And what should her reaction be?

Mo interrupted her thoughts asking, "Does Mike's drinking have to do just with Jimmy and Marie and the Torellis, Meg, or does it run deeper than that?"

Meg shrugged, shook her head, and said, "Well you heard him; it's part of his cultural fabric. Although, sometimes he seems to be intimidated—or maybe a little jealous—about his sister's wealthy circumstances. I don't know."

During their meal, attention focused on Jimmy and the television shows he liked to watch. That went quickly, and talk shifted to the dogs and cats owned by the various other tenants in the apartment building.

Mo told about a parrot she and her husband had owned years before and how Meg had taught it to say, "Spaghetti, please." Jimmy at first thought they were kidding him but, finally convinced, deftly turned the story into the basis for a compliment by asking, "Why spaghetti instead of Meg's delicious lasagna?" There were appreciative chuckles over that, and Mo explained that was long before Meg had learned to cook.

Through most of this, Mike had become quieter. This was partly because of the attention he, too, was paying to Jimmy, but probably mostly because of the attention he was paying to the Chianti wine Meg had offered at the table.

Suddenly Mike said to Jimmy, "Hey, I thought you were going to ask Meg about the little people." Mo looked up at him sharply, because the word "ask" sounded to her more like "ashk." Mike caught Mo's glance and, realizing his mispronunciation, flushed with embarrassment.

"Excuse me, Mo. I meant to say, 'ask.' I'm not that bad." Then Mike turned to Meg and said, "Go ahead. Tell him one of your stories about the 'little people.'"

"Yes, yes, Meg," Jimmy said. "And use your Irish...Irish as-cent. Daddy said you would do it."

"Go ahead, Meg. I'll help Mo with the dishes." Leaving Meg and Jimmy at the dining table, Mike gathered up their plates, utensils, and what remained of the Chianti and preceded Mo along the three or four steps into the kitchen. He put the dishes in the sink, and then slid onto one of the two stools tucked under a serving/sandwich counter and said, "I'll dry, Mo; just point me at a dish towel." With that he reached for the wine and poured it into one of the wine glasses Mo had brought from the table. Mo handed Mike a towel and said, "How about coffee instead, Mike?" She was quiet.

"Don't you worry, Mo; just point me at a dish towel."

Sighing, Mo turned to the dishes and leftovers and a minute later was startled to hear the harsh scrape of Mike's stool as he pushed it back from the counter, stood, and lurched through the door to the living room.

"Siddown a minute," he said, and Meg watched him weave to the sofa and sprawl on his back into a cushioned corner.

CHAPTER NINE

Jimmy had briefly seen his father's exit from the kitchen but was far too enchanted with Meg's Irish lore about "the wee folk" to have noticed what had happened after that. Meg was aware though, and simply kept up a stream of stories and anecdotes until her mother joined the two of them.

She had brought Jimmy's Game Boy and said, "Try this for a while, Jimmy. Poor Meg must be all talked out."

"No she's not. Meg's kissed the Blarney Stone, and she's got the 'gift of gab.' She told me. But I want to be polite, so okay."

Meg and Mo thought that was about the funniest thing they'd heard and spontaneously giggled hilariously while Jimmy slumped over his screen, his fingers jabbing the game to life.

"Now what?"

Meg returned her mother's exasperated, concerned, questioning look with her palms upturned. "I don't know. What happened?"

"Like a light switch. Sharp as a tack then dull as a brick in two minutes. He must reach a threshold he's not even aware of and bam!"

"Was he nasty?"

"Of course not—sweet as pie...wanted to dry the dishes...forgot I'd tossed him a towel...then teeter-totterville. The lights went out."

"Mom, he knows about this. Otherwise he'd have been a heck of a lot more defensive before. I mean this is a sensitive area for anyone—even a d-r-u-n-k. And he's not even close to that."

She spelled the word drunk and that distracted Jimmy from his Game Boy. "Where's Daddy?" he said.

"He was really tired, Jimmy, and Aunt Mo and I thought a little nap on the couch after that big lasagna would be just right." Meg winked at her mom. "In fact, we thought it might be a fun idea for him to just curl up for the night, right where he is and for you to sleep over too—in the guest room."

"Really, Meg?" Jimmy's eyes lit up. "Daddy would like that, and so would I. But where will you sleep?"

Good question, Meg thought. Then, "Oh, I have to go home Jimmy. You and your dad stay here at Aunt Mo's, and then you can go home in the morning. How about tucking in now?"

That was resolved a lot more easily than both women would have thought, and within fifteen minutes Jimmy was falling asleep in the guest bedroom. Mo had pulled out a flannel night shirt, without bottoms, which Jimmy agreed would be acceptable since that's the way his father slept. A fresh toothbrush was located, prayers said, and goodnight kisses were exchanged. As the ladies backed out of the room, Jimmy whispered, "Aunt Mo? Please kiss Daddy goodnight for me."

Mo had draped a comforter over Mike while Meg was supervising Jimmy's prayers, and they could hear Mike's muffled snores as they quietly crossed through the darkened living room to the kitchen. Meg closed the louvered doors and poured two cups of coffee left over from dinner. "It can't be easy," she said.

"Nope, and it's not going to be easy. What do you think?" asked Mo.

"About this, or about Jimmy?"

"Well, I was thinking about Jimmy. This could be simply a relieved collapse amidst the protective security of people who are fond of you.

After what he's dealt with this week he doesn't need an excuse to cave in."

"That's nice, Mom. I agree, but I do think he's pushing a little too hard on the Scotch. This didn't start at the wake you know; I've known Mike a long time, and so have you. What about Jimmy?"

"I could just love him to death, he's so sweet. Have you ever seen manners like his in a child that age? Did you hear him call me Aunt Mo before?" Mo's eyes were misting with a hint of tears. "I'd like to take care of him."

"Would you? You mean here instead of daycare?"

"Well sure," Mo said. "He's head-over-heels in love with us—don't know how we could be so lucky; we've known Mike a long time. He needs the help. I'm tired of being lonely. I'd love caring for Jimmy."

"Oh, Mom. Oh, Mom!" Meg threw her arms around her mother and pulled her close. "You are the angel Jimmy was praying for. It's you." And gently they both let their tears go.

CHAPTER TEN

Mo awoke at ten after five o'clock Tuesday morning when she heard Mike groping about in the living room. Knowing he might be confused, she walked into the hall to meet him, pulling on her robe as she went.

Before Meg had left, the two of them had considered the best and most reassuring way to put Mike at ease when he awoke, and Mo spoke first, as they had decided. "You deserved a full night's sleep, Mike, and so did Jimmy. Good morning!"

"Thanks, Mo. That's nice, but I don't think I've behaved very well passing out on you. Where's Jimmy?"

"Shhh. He's still asleep in the guest room, Mike. Not to worry. He's a good little guest, and you're a good guest too. So not another word. The bathroom is down on the left. You can share Jimmy's toothbrush. It's the green one. Meanwhile, I'll put some coffee on for us."

Mo looked in on Jimmy while the coffee was perking, and she flushed with the love she felt for him. Still sound, sound asleep, he was curled in a tight ball with an apparent smile on his face. *We're so lucky*, she thought.

Mike was bright-eyed, but sheepish, when he entered the kitchen. But he didn't look as rumpled as one would expect from having spent the night on the couch.

"Thanks for putting us up, Mo." Mike leaned over and kissed the top of her head, then joined her at the counter where Mo had set out orange juice, coffee, and toasted bagels. "I'm about as embarrassed as anyone could be. First I pour out all my troubles, then I drink all your..."

"Mike, you can do things like that when you're with people who love you. It's like family—people forgive lapses. So let's talk about happy things."

"Hmmm. That's nice, Mo. You know, I do feel love for you and Meg. Think of that...all these years."

"Well, that's really nice. Thank you. So, what's today's schedule like?"

"I don't know, Mo. I'll have to get Jimmy into some fresh clothes and check out the daycare centers near our place. One calls itself 'The Prep School.' Can you imagine that? Anyway, I'll be taking days off until I can sort this out."

"Meg and I've got a better idea, Mike. We don't like what we hear about 'daycares.' And even if we did I'd still like to care for Jimmy myself. How does that sound to you? I really mean it."

"You're kidding!"

"Not kidding. I want to take care of Jimmy. And not just for him and you—for me too, and for Meg. It would mean a new life for me—for us. I'm still young enough."

"Well of course you are. Of course I, uh, I just can't believe it. And besides..."

"Think about it, Mike. As for my rates, they'll be practically nothing compared with daycare centers; just enough to make it reasonable for both of us. Try it out for a few days, or a week, and give yourself and Jimmy some time. Just try it for today, if you want. Of course Jimmy's the client; we'd have to see if he likes the idea."

"Mo. Mo. Mo. You're so good. When I think that my own family; my in-laws...well, and you...! That's what loving is all about." He reached his arms around her and gently hugged.

"Excuse me."

Hearing his son's voice, Mike relaxed his embrace around Mo's shoulders and, grinning broadly, turned in the direction of Jimmy's all-too-polite interruption.

"Faith and begorra, me lad. Is it you out of yer bed at this early hour? And I'm supposin' yer likely hungry, too? Will ye be having some tea, lad? Here, give us a kiss!"

Jimmy shrieked with delight and rushed to be included in the embrace with his father and Mo. "You sound just like the little people, Daddy. Meg said that's the brogue."

"Irish brogue it is, young man. Takes a lot of practice. Good morning, Jimmy."

"Good morning. That was fun last night, Mo."

"It *was* fun. Thanks for coming. How did you sleep?"

"Like a block of...of what, Daddy?" Jimmy said.

"Of wood."

"Like a block of wood, Aunt Mo. Daddy's right. I'm hungry."

After their brief breakfast (Mo served Jimmy the Sugar Pops he chose and Mike enjoyed another bagel), Mike said, "Jimmy, while I'm at work how would you like to spend your days right here with Aunt Mo?"

Unbelievably, Jimmy said, "Faith and begorra. Really?"

And he convulsed in laughter, which grew all the more hysterical as Mike began to tickle his ribs until Jimmy sagged to his knees and wriggled free.

"Yes, really." Mo said. "Your daddy and I think, and Meg agrees, everyone would have more fun and feel better and happier if we all stuck together. What do you think?"

"What about Daddy? Would I ever get to see him?" Jimmy's chin was quivering.

Mike quickly swept Jimmy up onto his lap. "Oh Jimmy, we didn't explain it right. Don't worry; this would be only during the daytime. After breakfast at our house I will bring you here and come back to pick you up after work. And then we'll go home for the night."

"What about my toys?"

"Whatever you need will be right here, Jimmy. We'll make space for your things in the guest room. That's where you can take your naps, if you want, and stay in bed if you get sick."

"I'd like it, Aunt Mo. Are you sure, Daddy?"

"I am if you are, Jimmy. That's what I asked Aunt Mo, and she's sure, too."

Mo and Mike could see how excited Jimmy was, so the three of them made lists of things Jimmy wanted for starters. Then he and Mike left for their apartment to wash up and change clothes and to gather the prerequisite toys, books, and games. They returned to Mo's about eight-thirty in plenty of time for Mike to get to the television station reasonably on time.

Mo told Jimmy they would start their day with a story and asked him to sort out his books and things in the guest room.

"Have fun, Jimmy. I'll call later to see how you are. Here's a kiss." Mike turned to Mo on the way out. "Mo, if it turns out that this is absolutely the worst idea, tell me right away. You're taking on an awful lot, and I'd rather keep visiting for dinners than never seeing the Donlons again."

"Don't give it a thought, Mike. But thank you. I can't wait to start planning things to do. Now you go to work and tell Meg right away. She's anxious."

"Uh oh. Did I do something terrible last night? I mean beyond acting like a bum?"

"Not at all. I would have told you. Meg's anxious, because she's a part of this too, Mike—a big part. She'll want to know what you and Jimmy decided—first hand. So go see her right away. Remember, you were going to take the day off, so now you've got time to do the important things first. I hope this doesn't sound like a speech."

"Nope. Good advice. Love you, Mo. Any problems just..."

"Call you. Right."

"Yup. See you at five-thirty."

CHAPTER ELEVEN

The drive to Channel 5 from Mo's involved a quarter mile on an access road to I-95, another quarter mile jump on and off the interstate, and a two minute, right, right, left, left combination to get to the station. Maybe ten minutes.

But it was close to nine o'clock, and the morning rush hour still produced moderately heavy traffic. Also, the New York to Boston tractor-trailer crawl was reaching a peak that would sustain through the evening.

So Mike's quick trip turned to a dead stop the moment he got on I-95 and, like a slap, he realized that Monday's traumatic events had completely distracted him from thoughts of visiting his wife's grave.

I've got to go, he thought. *Oh Marie, I miss you too. So does Jimmy. But what do you think about Mo Donlon? Isn't this wonderful for Jimmy?*

To get to the East Haven cemetery meant staying on the interstate for another two miles over the notoriously backed-up "Q" Bridge. From where he was he could see that nothing was moving, so he changed his mind about a visit with Marie and slowly eased into a left exit to get to his job.

Once in his office, a quick glance at his desk confirmed Michelle's

Monday afternoon report that things had been quiet. There were just three pink telephone slips—one from Dave Batchelder and the others from clients. All could wait.

Mike buzzed Meg's office, and he could sense her anxiety when she picked up the phone. "Hey, it's your couch potato from last night. Good morning, Meg. Are you busy?"

"Nope. Come on over, and please bring me a fresh coffee if you're stopping by the kitchen." She was relieved at Mike's fairly believable attempt at nonchalance.

Mike sheepishly kissed Meg's cheek, offered another apology to her, and told her how well it had gone with Jimmy after Mo had told him the decision she and Meg had come to after dinner. Then he thanked her, for himself and Jimmy.

Meg's eyes sparkled with pleasure at Mike's delight and Jimmy's easy acceptance of the new arrangement. And she chuckled to hear her mother's protest about being young enough to take on what Meg knew would be a pleasure to her. The two of them chattered away for nearly an hour before Michelle's call asking if Mike had a few minutes for Dave.

As Mike rose to get back to business, Meg said, "How about a nice lunch today?"

"Sure. Phelan's okay?"

"That's okay, but how about the new coffee house next door. The Beanery?"

"You're on," said Mike. "Lobby at noon."

* * * * *

When Dave stepped into Mike's office to talk, Mike felt embarrassed for his well intentioned but illogical attempt to rationalize the position Dave had promoted the day before. So after a few minutes of back-pedaling double-talk and pats on the back, Dave apologized for the final time and with a dopey, lopsided grin, said, "Attaboy, go get 'em. Thanks for your support." After Dave had gone, Mike slowly shook his head and thought, *Why is it that I'm working for that dope?*

* * * * *

As Meg and Mike entered The Beanery, Mike's mental alarm had already begun to ring. For one thing, there were no neon lights in the windows merchandising his favorite beers; he had already dismissed that with the hopeful expectation that this place was too upscale for that. But when the doors opened, all he could smell was the aroma of coffee beans—rich, dramatic, chic, and loathsome. *My God,* he thought. *This place is as dry as Murphy's well. What am I going to do?*

Turning to Meg he said, "No bar, huh?"

"It's only lunchtime, Mike. There's plenty of time for drinks at happy hour. We can go to Phelan's then."

"That's right. Well, that's okay, Meg. It's just that I wish I had known. I sort of look forward to a drink or a beer. But it's okay. Coffee's okay."

After a cup of delicious, fresh, "mountain-side," Colombian coffee, Mike's jangling, alcohol-aching nerves flattened out, and he was surprised—actually pleased—that this wasn't so bad after all. He thought, in fact, that it was pretty good. His breathing slowed to a near-normal pace, his jitters faded, he felt at one with the other patrons. *I am,* he thought, *more of a bon vivant than I ever thought. How civilized!*

And Meg's initial nervousness dissipated as she watched and felt Mike relax. She purposely hadn't told him this was a dry restaurant, because she wanted him to be fully alert to what she wanted to discuss.

They ordered what Mike thought was about the goofiest food he'd ever heard of—sliced cucumbers on toast points with pate on the side (appetizer); grilled (in virgin olive oil) Tofu sandwiches with a side of bean sprouts sprinkled with red vinegar. *Or was it vinaigrette?* he thought. "Meg, this is kind of nice. I like this stuff. A little hoity-toity, maybe; do you think they'd let me in if you weren't with me?"

"During the week I think. I'm not sure about the weekends." Meg grinned, and Mike grinned back.

"I expected Mo might have called this morning," Mike said. "I guess it's working."

"It will. Jimmy's such a stable youngster. It'll be great for both of them. And for you too, I hope."

"You're antsy, Meg. What's on your mind? Last night was a mistake, and I don't make mistakes too often."

"I know. And I'm sort of relieved to know that you're aware that you drink a little too much; maybe more often than you'd like."

Mike looked up sharply. "How do you know that?"

"You told us last night, Mike. That's why I told Mom you were all right...because you were in control. But you can be in more control."

"Oh. How does that happen?"

"Well what about right now? You're in a coffee bar. And it's not so bad, right?"

"No, it's fine. Could probably use a bit more gravy on the Tofu, but sure, it's fine."

"Well?"

"Maybe I shouldn't have brought up that scolding from my brother-in-law. I told you because I need someone on my side, but that doesn't seem to be happening."

"Mike, listen to me. My father was an alcoholic. He was a great man; a great father. But he was a drunk. And his jokes and good times and buddies and booze killed him. And Mom and I just watched it happen."

"Jesus, Meg. How'd I know...?"

"Mike, you wouldn't know. Nobody would know. Nobody ever knows about stuff like that—or child abuse or wife beating. But guess what? It's all around you—us, me. And we let it happen. And you know what that's called? Enabling. We grin and say it's okay; that's just the way it is with old Frank or Betsy or Charlie or Mike. And we have our own drinks, too, one for one, right along with them until Frank, Betsy, Charlie, and Mike all fall down."

"Or pass out on the couch."

"Okay. Pass out on the couch."

"Meg, I'm sorry about your dad."

"Everyone was—all his friends, the priests, the entire family. And the next day they're all gone, and it's just Mom and me looking at each other and bawling our heads off asking each other how we let it happen. Goddamnit!"

Mike jerked back at Meg's vehement blasphemy. He'd never heard her swear before, and he was shaken. And he felt helpless as she started to sob and shake—right there. Tears ran down her cheeks, and nearby patrons didn't know what to think.

"Meg. Hold my hands, Meg. It's okay. Hold my hands."

And she did, and the sobs heaved up in her all the more, and Mike moved into the chair next to her and put his right arm around her and pulled her close to him. "It's okay, Meg. I'll take care of you. Shhh. It's okay. I'll take care of me, too."

"Oh Mike. I love you and Jimmy so much. Thank you. Please understand. I'm not a complainer. You're just too good to go away."

"I'm not going away, Meg. Not from you and Mo and Jimmy. I promise."

CHAPTER TWELVE

Meg and Mike had trouble finishing their lunch orders and finally gave up picking and pushing the remains around their plates. They even declined their waiter's multiple offers of more coffee and decided to skip dessert. Meg managed to nudge things back on track, when Mike snapped up the bill, by saying, "I'm hosting this, remember? I invited you." All this was over Mike's stern but subdued protestation, but he grinned. And then he got a grin out of Meg when he jokingly asked for her receipt so he could submit it with his weekly expense account.

During their stroll back to the station, Meg decided to skip the rest of her work day to see how Mo and Jimmy were doing. As Mike walked her to her car, parked in the lot behind the station, Meg clutched his arm saying, "Mike, I'm upset I was so direct. You're really entitled to much more trust from me than that."

"It's okay, Meg. It's really okay. You said the right things...for all of us. Wait and see. See what Mo says; she'll agree with me too and support what you did."

"I know she will, Mike. But what about you? Really?"

"I've got to agree with you; because you're right, and because I want to.

It'll be tough, but I'm going to be better. And I love you, too." He kissed her on the lips, and they embraced for as long as they dared out in the open.

Back in his office, Mike realized how shaken he was, and it took him a good half-hour staring at the studio television monitor to regain a reasonable level of calm. But his emotions kept running to Meg's unexpected, and seemingly sincere, disclosure of love for him and Jimmy. Once said though, it seemed so obvious and natural. As if, well, what else? And then how easy it had been for him to tell Meg he loved her—and to kiss. He grinned to himself thinking, *Who would have thought after all these years? Like falling in love with the little kid next door whom you had always ignored.*

Flushed with his sudden confidence, Mike keyed the monitor's volume down and buzzed Michelle for his messages. She suddenly appeared in his office door rather than picking up the receiver, and Mike blushed thinking she may have glimpsed him and Meg outside.

Michelle's bubbly good humor, to his relief, derived from the message she had for him. "This is a big one, Mike. *OutFront Sportwear* called with a huge order. Charlie Martin called himself. They picked up your entire proposal and wanted commercial time on Oprah, too."

"No way."

"Yes! And I've cleared it with traffic and fixed up this e-mail for Dave."

"Wow! Why an e-mail?"

"Otherwise he might start thinking he's the guy who got the order!" They both laughed at that.

"That's smart, Michelle. You know you're pretty smart for..."

"Don't say it, you."

Mike finished the sentence, "...for the number one sales associate in the Hartford/New Haven ADI."

"Oh. You really think so?" Michelle was flustered.

"Of course. Well, maybe that's a little generous, but, yeah, you're the best for a..."

At that Michelle feinted a flanking move around Mike's desk

pretending to smack him, but he held out his hand to shake hers and said, "I really do think so! You are. And thanks."

"I told Charlie you would be out to see him today and he said, 'Any time you want.'"

"Thanks, star! Send Dave the e-mail, and fax the confirmation to Charlie. Wow! Anything else?"

"Yeah, your lips are red; who would kiss someone like you at lunch? Yuck."

Mike flushed bright red, recovered, and made a step in Michelle's direction, but she was down the hall, laughing out loud.

* * * * *

OutFront Sportwear was east of New Haven in Branford, the town just beyond East Haven. And after Mike finished his celebratory meeting with his client, he drove to East Lawn Cemetery.

The drive was a pretty one along US Route 1, the famous Boston Post Road, and Mike found it easy to attend to the traffic and still let his mind wander to events over the past two days.

I guess I over-reacted with Dave, he thought. *That scene with Fran and Thomas at Marie's grave must have hit me harder than I thought. But how about Mo stepping in when Meg gave her the word? And what a jerk you are...passing out like a fool. Thanks, Marie. I know you're watching out for us...even though I was the one who promised. I'll cut back on the sauce, too. It used to upset you. Now my sister's worried. Meg really has a right to be angry. Oh, okay. Maybe she doesn't. Not yet, anyway. And that was an innocent kiss, Marie. Of course I couldn't possibly love her. I love what she's doing—and Mo, too. And you know I love you.*

Mike had reached the cemetery and parked just inside the gate. Now, with tears welling in his eyes, he started the car and re-parked by the path that led past Jimmy's little angel. Fresh flowers had been left there since Sunday, and he assumed they had come from the Torellis. "An apology, maybe? Hey, if they really can't handle Jimmy, give them credit for telling me now. What the hell. And look—hasn't it worked out the way it should have?" The flowers were nice. More of the roses Marie had loved.

"Okay, Marie. I can't promise to get off the booze completely, because I don't know if I can do it. But I'm going to try." More tears came as he said a brief prayer, then drove away.

Outside, he deliberately drove right past Phelan's Bar and straight to Mo's to pick up his son. Mo would realize this was a big first step.

CHAPTER THIRTEEN

The next few weeks were like a rebirth for Mike. Marie's spiritual presence was nearly always with Mike, but that didn't inhibit him. It was a good time. He was able to share with her spirit the happiness Jimmy was experiencing and over and over express his gratitude for Mo stepping in.

He was particularly free of the burdens he had expected to have to contend with in trying to provide for Jimmy's care. And that meant not just the effort of trying to locate Jimmy in a wholesome, caring facility, but coping with the fear that problems would develop anyway. All of this, he knew, would lead to the guilt he would suffer if he weren't able to keep his promises to Marie. That was the worst— feeling he would be letting Marie down. This guilt was part of his Irish-Catholic heritage—his Boston-Irish-Catholic heritage.

And Jimmy *was* happy. Not the soft, mushy, sweet, mother/child happy, but still plenty happy. Mo sent him off every night with new information about the world around him and with new adventures from the stories they read together. He began to keep a booklet containing words he was learning to read and write. And it seemed he was coming away with a growing self-confidence. Mainly he had gone beyond the tears of sorrow for his mother, and when he did cry, usually at prayers, they were happy tears.

With Meg it was a different story. For a few days after their lunch, she had withdrawn, and Mike, thinking she was embarrassed over their kiss and professions of love, let it go. There was a lot going on with increased advertising volume, which kept them both busy, and they had just a few minutes for coffee together each morning.

One night, Mo offered Mike a drink when he arrived to pick up Jimmy, and she was impressed when he declined. "Good for you, Mike. Meg told me about your lunch; she really feels terribly."

"Because I kissed her?"

"Oh?" Mo was clearly startled. "No, Mike. Meg didn't mention that." She smiled. "How lovely." Mike blushed. "No. Meg felt she was way out of line, and told me that afterwards she felt you must have thought she was a scolding nag. She's been mortified for a week."

"So that's it. I thought she was embarrassed by my behavior over here after dinner, and then I made it worse by being forward. She's right about my drinking. I'll call her tonight," Mike said. "I was just giving her time to forgive me for my problem. And it looks like my problem has led to another one."

* * * * *

On the way home with Jimmy, Mike found himself rehearsing the phone conversation he could have with Meg when he thought, *God, this is ridiculous. I've known her almost ten years...why do I have to practice what I'm going to say to her?* "What's going on here?"

The last four words were said aloud, and Jimmy, who'd been quietly browsing the pages of a new picture book, looked up. "What, Daddy?"

Mike grinned at the opportunity to pull another of the pranks he shared with his son. "I just said, 'What's wrong over there?'" and he pointed in front of Jimmy out the passenger window.

As usual, Jimmy asked, "Where?" and quickly turned his head to look.

At that moment, Mike withdrew his pointed finger and used it, instead, to poke Jimmy on the back of his neck saying, "Got you again!" laughing uproariously while he did it. Jimmy yelped and used all ten fingers to repeatedly poke his father in his right bicep while Mike said, "No, Jimmy. Look. Look! Oh, too bad. Don't miss it."

At this, Jimmy said, "I'm not looking ever again."

Mike used to try and pull the prank on Marie, and it took the very young Jimmy a couple of years to catch on. They always laughed.

* * * * *

After dinner, when Jimmy had been asleep at least an hour, Mike called Meg, and they talked softly but intensely for a long time, and after that it was all right. Neither said a thing about love or kisses or drinking, and Mike couldn't tell if she had spoken to Mo or not. He was sure she had, but he couldn't tell. That was nice.

The outcome was their agreement to just let things get back to where they were; coffee in the morning at the station, if they could, and lunch next week at The Beanery.

CHAPTER FOURTEEN

Mike's birthday was June 11; also the anniversary date of his 1988 marriage and its approach had troubled Mike. The guilt again, for reasons that made sense not only to him but to Meg as well. They decided to simply enjoy an early dinner at Mo's with Jimmy and restrict beverages to soft drinks and water. Mike tucked away his recollections of his wedding day and found he felt refreshingly innocent, and they all enjoyed the small party.

Mike and Jimmy made regular visits to Marie's gravesite, and these were part of planned visits to afterwards see Maman and Papa and the girls when they were home. Mike's calls to thank them for their grave flowers seemed to have broken the tension, and they were happy about the arrangements with Mo. It seemed to Mike, however, that Fran was a bit miffed hearing how easy it had been to replace her as Jimmy's caregiver, but he just let that go. *Now that Marie's an angel she can get stuff done*, he had said to himself.

Occasionally Carmen or Regina would call Mike and offer to babysit on weekends, and this was good for everyone. They were able to stay in close touch with Jimmy, and Mike and Meg were able to go out by themselves more frequently. One night, Mike got home to find that Fran had come over to relieve Regina, who had suddenly felt feverish and didn't want to expose Jimmy to a bug.

"What a nice surprise, Fran. I didn't know this was a team effort. Is everything okay?"

"Regina wasn't well, Mike, so I was able to read Jimmy a couple of stories, listen to his prayers, and kiss him goodnight. I enjoyed it. And I've been wondering if you two would like to join us for the eleven o'clock Mass next week and visit Marie afterwards. Then you could come back to the house for one of those big, Italian Sunday dinners I used to make."

This was a stunning reversal for Mike of Fran and Thomas's still unexpected and unexplained decision to renege on their promise that he and Marie would never have to worry about Jimmy. *I'll bet they're afraid it was too easy for Jimmy and me to just shift gears and move on with our lives, thanks to Mo. But what caused them to tell me they couldn't 'take Jimmy' in the first place? Did they blame Marie's cancer on me, or something equally foolish?* He couldn't figure it out and jumped over it with, "Fran, that will be great. Jimmy and I can't wait."

So Mass and Sunday dinner it was, and everyone was not only astonished at Jimmy's recognition of most of the different dishes, but also amazed at how he dug into the food and sampled a bit of every course from the antipasto through the bracciole, and finally the spumoni for dessert. The containers of leftovers Fran packed for them to take home lasted for days.

* * * * *

At the station, Mike was arriving early and putting in the same extended hours, but he was enjoying the work more and getting more work done. And his interpersonal relations seemed to be much more stable; no more cranky outbursts of temper; he was far more patient with occasional staff shortcomings, and he actually found himself in tune with some of Dave Batchelder's even more eccentric points of view. Others recognized this too, but only he and Meg realized why. And Mike, himself, was astounded and ashamed that cutting back on his drinking could have yielded such a dramatic and measurable effect. *What a Goddamn fool I've been*, he thought.

Another measurable outcome was his productivity as defined by increased sales and billings. This, of course, produced a jump in Mike's commission income which, as good as he knew he was, impressed even him. He started to save more and more money and it made him feel he had reached a new level not only in his work ethic but also in his life.

He and Meg had also reached a new level. While they always interacted professionally inside the station, their at least once or twice-weekly lunches at The Beanery soon identified them as an "item." Their decorum was perfect, but the intensity of their conversations made it clear they were on subjects far more important than the new lineup of network TV shows scheduled for the coming fall.

For nighttime entertainment they went to the movies once a week, usually a week night and either a weekend lunch, which Jimmy enjoyed with them as well, or a dinner out on Friday or Saturday night. If it was a movie night, they always went to Phelan's afterwards where Mike had just one beer. He loved being there with Tim and Heather and all the other regulars, and he loved being in control of himself. If it was for lunch, then just club soda (no lime). For dinner Mike allowed himself one Scotch whisky, on the rocks; no wine, no beer, no liqueurs.

"I'm so proud of you, Mike. You said you were going to do it and you have. You're wonderful!"

This was at one of their lunches at The Beanery, and it was Meg's frequent statements of praise which not only caused Mike to redden with pleasure, but reinforced what he was pledged to and renewed his determination.

"It's true that I'm getting to know a lot about coffee, that's for sure. But you're the wonderful one, Meg, enticing me here in the first place. And I'm learning so much more about you!"

Meg smiled back and changed the subject. "What have you heard from your sister and family? They seem to have fallen out of touch."

"I spoke with Mary a couple of weeks ago when I called to wish Martha a happy birthday. She turned fourteen on July 15. They're all okay. Tom called me back that night to catch up on things. I guess they're at Marblehead now, sailing and whatever else they do. I haven't been invited up there in years."

Marblehead, Massachusetts, on the so-called "north shore" of Boston, had long been a favorite vacation spot for New England's upper crust. The south shore, on the other hand, which descended south of Boston and out to Cape Cod, had always been considered the alternative for the non-elite. Those distinctions had blurred, perhaps vanished, over the years, but descendants of Brahmins sometimes couldn't let it go. Mike could and had; his sister probably never would.

"I'd like to get together with the Dickinson family," Mike said. "It bothers me that they just dropped out of sight after the funeral. And, I'm sensitive about that scolding from Tom."

"But you don't have to worry about that anymore, Mike. You're fine. You *should* get together. It's important for Jimmy, too."

"What do you think about a picnic on Labor Day weekend, Meg? We could all get together at a beach somewhere. That would be easy for everyone."

"And it's neutral, Mike."

"That's why the picnic, Meg. The Torellis should be there too, with Carmen and Regina. And you and Mo of course."

This startled Meg, and she gasped involuntarily. "Oh no, Mike. That wouldn't be right. No one would be ready for that. Why Labor Day would be only four months after Marie died."

"Meg, Jimmy wouldn't have survived without Mo and her love. And I wouldn't have survived without you. You're both part of *my* family." Mike wanted to say he couldn't have survived without Meg's love, but this wasn't the time for that. "And they've got to understand that. Think what people would wonder about if Jimmy was upset because of your absence."

In the end, Mike's idea seemed to be a good one, and Meg began to make lists of the snacks, salads, and desserts Mike could ask the others to bring. They would supply the burgers, hot dogs, and beverages. And they agreed the best place would be at Hammonassett State Park.

Hammonassett was well known for what most visitors called the nicest beach between the New Jersey shore and Cape Cod. It was located fifteen or twenty miles east of New Haven, in the town of Clinton, and would take the Dickinsons only about forty-five minutes to get there from their home in Farmington. Mainly, though, the picnic facilities were great, with tables and grills, and the pavilions offered plenty of showers and restroom facilities.

That night, when Meg told her mother about the plans, Mo agreed and, with a chuckle, said, "Introducing you to the family? Sounds good to me."

"You too, Mom." Meg said. "Mike says you and I *are* part of the family. So maybe the others are being introduced to us."

CHAPTER FIFTEEN

"...we can't come to the phone right now, but if you leave a message we'll call you back soon."

Mike responded, "Who belongs to this grown-up voice I'm hearing? Is that you on the answering machine, Barbara? Wow...maybe you should be a reporter on the evening news."

Barbara was Mary and Tom Dickinson's older child and would turn sixteen a few weeks into September. *She really did sound mature*, Mike thought.

"It's your Uncle Mike, and I thought you'd all be back from vacation by now. You've got my number, so call when..."

"Mike, it's Tom. Don't hang up. How are you?"

"Fine, thanks. Are you home from Marblehead already?"

"Mary and the girls are still up there, Mike. I had to get back for some court dates, but I'll be returning Friday night. How are you? Want to go back up with me?"

"Jimmy and I could use a break like that, Tom, but not this year. We still have lots of adjusting. But thanks."

"Is everything okay?"

"Oh sure. I'm calling to ask you all to a Labor Day weekend picnic Jimmy and I are having. So when you see Mary, ask her to check the calendar."

"That sounds great. Mary will probably call you back this weekend. Where's it going to be?"

"We'll meet out at Hammonassett if you can make it. I'm going to ask the Torellis, too."

"That's a great idea. We've always enjoyed it there. How's the job going?"

"Fine, Tom. Everything's fine. Jimmy's fine. It's good talking to you. Say hi to the girls."

After he rung off, Mike wondered if Tom's questions were probing for problems or if he was letting his imagination make a big deal over them. *He sounded genuine enough*, Mike thought. *Damn. I didn't even ask how the ladies are. And it's really odd that he didn't ask about Jimmy or how he was spending his days.*

Mike's sister called a couple days later though, and was embarrassingly apologetic over Tom's omission in general manners. "He'd been distracted with the litigation that dragged him away from Marblehead and wasn't even thinking, for God's sake. I keep telling him vacations mean no work."

"It's okay, Mary. Jimmy spends his days with an old friend of mine, Mo Donlon, who retired from the station just last fall. She was the receptionist, but I don't think you'd remember her. Tom might."

Mary had visited Channel 5 only a couple of times, mostly for network cocktail parties; at one time her husband stopped in regularly to visit Mike, but that was when their daughters were younger.

"How wonderful, Mike. Is that a daycare or what?"

"No, her apartment is out on New Haven Point and looks across Long Island Sound. She's a widow. Jimmy loves it there, and she loves him and loves taking care of him."

"I see. And you?"

"Me? Well of course Mo loves me, but not that way. We're sort of family. She'll be at the picnic, and so will her daughter, Meg. Oh, and now that I know you can make it, I'll ask the Torellis to make it an even dozen."

"Well that sounds wonderful, Mike. It will be nice to have the Donlons to balance out the Italian side of the family. What can I bring?"

For a moment Mike thought he would drop the phone. *"What the hell was that?"* he asked himself. He was about to slam down the phone but instead said, "I'm going to ask Meg to call you about that. It will probably be a salad or dessert, but you two can decide."

"Oh, good. How old is Meg?"

"In her thirties. I'm not sure." Mike certainly wasn't stepping into that trap. Of course he knew Meg's age, but Mary was moving in too closely, too soon. "Not much younger than you I'd say." *That ought to cut this line of questions short,* he thought.

And it did. Mary thanked him again for the invite and said she'd look forward to Meg's call. Her girls would be so excited, and she couldn't wait and so on. Mike could tell her antennae were twitching with intrigue as they said goodnight.

Mary called back a few minutes later. "You remember that Mom and Dad always spend Labor Day weekend with us, Mike. They're invited, too, aren't they?"

In fact, Mike had forgotten about that annual visit and stammered an apology. Their parents had moved to the Boston suburb of Wellesley a couple of years before, and that was an easy detour for Michael and Gail Flynn on their way home from Marblehead to Farmington. "Of course, Mary, I feel like a dope. Sorry. How are they? Have they been up to Marblehead yet?"

"Last weekend. And they're fine. This will be a nice treat for them."

Mike's dad was a young sixty-seven and over his working years had become self-pitying because of his inability to get promoted to the level of success he hoped to achieve. He kept assuring himself that it was only a matter of time before his reporting skills would propel him into the city editor's office but, in fact, he had only a short stint at the political editor's desk before going back on the beat. The problem was he couldn't manage people, or motivate them, and he wasn't cut out to be anything more than a beat reporter. He could write though, and the *Herald* valued him for that. So at age sixty-four he took an early retirement, moved to Wellesley with Gail, and groused long-distance about "the crap you see in the papers these days."

Mike hadn't been able to maintain closeness with either of his folks over the past dozen years and relegated that familial necessity to his sister. His mother, the former society editor, relished boasting to her neighbors about her daughter's Marblehead home, probably more than the visits she made there. His dad always seemed jealous that he'd never been able to achieve a semblance of his wife's success in her early years with the society column. His frequent emission of long, exasperated sighs, though, seemed to help him get over that.

When Marie was alive, it was she who kept in touch with Mike's parents by calling once or twice a week and sending birthday cards and occasional holiday greetings. Mike had spoken to his mother only once since Marie's funeral, and that was in a short call responding to a message she had left on his home answering machine.

Realizing full well that his parents never cared for the Torellis, and openly showed it sometimes, Mike couldn't agree with his sister that the visit would, in fact, be "nice" for them, but he said, "Of course it will, Mary. Would you mention it to Mom when you talk to her?"

"I will but not 'til the last minute. I don't want her to try to outdo Maman Fran in the 'favorite recipe' department. God, she's a pain sometimes."

Mike couldn't agree more but simply said, "I know. Thanks, Mary," and they rang off.

He immediately thought about Jimmy's assertion that Marie had told him the Dickinsons were bad people because they "didn't like 'Talians'" and realized that could actually be true given his mother's disturbing prejudice, which must have rubbed off onto his sister. Could it be that the

Torellis' reneging on their promise had been to get even for that? Hard to believe and he hoped not true. *God. What the hell do we have all this nonsense for?* he wondered.

The Torellis were equally enthusiastic when Mike spoke with Fran an hour later. But as Mike expected, she insisted that everyone convene in the Torellis' backyard. "Mike, we've got a pool, the gas grill, real toilets. Don't be crazy. Who goes to Hammonassett, anyway? The poor people, that's who."

Mike thought, *How do poor people fit into this?* but instead he said, "Fran, you've got the nicest yard in East Haven, except there's no sand. We're going to the beach. Carmen and Regina use Hammonassett all the time."

"Suppose we run out of food. How do you get to the deli and back?"

"Meg's got that all planned, Maman, and you can make double your recipes just to be sure. She'll probably call you tomorrow."

Fran had already known about Meg from the get togethers they'd had after Mass and the big Italian feast they'd enjoyed, so there was no uncomfortable needling on that point.

"You sure Papa can't bring those steaks you love?"

"It's hamburgers and hot dogs, a real old-fashioned picnic, Fran. Have fun. Eat watermelon. Spit seeds. No steaks."

"I'll let you know, Mike. What's your mother going to bring?"

Oh, oh, Mike thought. *Now she's my 'mother' and not Gail. So Fran is just as competitive.* He lied. "Mom and Dad will be visiting Mary and her family, Fran, and I don't think Mom will be comfortable cooking in the Dickinson kitchen." He could imagine Fran's wicked grin of satisfaction and, as they ended their conversation, that somehow cheered him. As a final shot he said, "I know they'll be really disappointed if the Torellis aren't there. Love you, Maman."

CHAPTER SIXTEEN

Meg giggled when Mike told her about Fran Torelli's attempt to take charge of the picnic plans and at her attempt to set up some competition with Mike's mother. And they were both happy when Fran called a few days later to promise all the Torellis were looking forward to the gathering.

The next few weeks were busy on all fronts. Mo and Mike were involved with late arrangements for enrolling Jimmy in a kindergarten that would be convenient to Mo's apartment and Mike's office. The fall TV time-selling season was heating up at Channel 5, and the sales department was busy promoting new shows and working with clients in developing advertising schedules for the busy, post-Labor Day retail period. Meg had made lists of supplies and beverages the picnic group would need and had scouted out an area convenient to parking, the restroom facilities, and the beach. Fran, to cement her own role probably, had called several times to confirm the head count to ensure she would prepare enough food. After a couple more tries to dissuade Mike from Hammonasset, she gave up and, in fact, seemed to become a proponent of the plan. Even Carmen and Regina called, and Mike assigned them the job of bringing bags of ice and a couple picnic coolers.

The consideration of Jimmy's schooling was unexpected and exciting to all—Mike, Meg, Mo, and particularly, Jimmy. While he would turn five in October, the usual age to begin Kindergarten, Mike had thought he might have to hold him back a year. Jimmy was enrolled in a nursery school the year before, but Mike had to take him out a few weeks after Christmas, when Marie had really begun to decline.

That was a sadly disturbing time for all—particularly Jimmy, whose earlier delight and hopeful expectations were harshly dashed. He had cried for days, and Marie and Mike were doubly miserable.

How sad, Mike now thought, *how the Torellis had let them down then, in the days Marie was too ill and Mike needed to be with her.* They had volunteered to chauffeur Jimmy to the school and care for him afterwards, but then backed away. They had reasons that made doing that impossible, except for a schedule that just didn't fit with the school's hours.

As for Jimmy's aptitude, however, Mike had discovered over that single term that his precocity was rooted in an impressive intelligence that manifested itself more every day. And with the alphabet and word exercises he and Jimmy enjoyed together, and with Marie when she was able, it was clear Jimmy was up to the mental challenge and, in fact, might be ahead of his classmates. His social maturity was another non-issue given Jimmy's interactive extroversion and charm. In seeking approval to enter Kindergarten, the several teachers who interviewed Jimmy confirmed Mike's assessment, and he was easily accepted.

With this happy resolution, it was difficult for Jimmy to contain his excitement during the last weeks of August. Mo took him shopping for school clothes, as well as for a new play outfit for the picnic. Labor Day was on September 4th that year, and Jimmy's first day of school was a few days earlier, on Thursday. It was hard to tell who was prouder when the three of them walked into the Franklin School (a few blocks from Mo's place) and into Jimmy's classroom.

The plan was for Mo to pick Jimmy up at noon when school was over, feed him lunch, and then wait for Mike to come by in the evening from work. On opening day though, Mo had invited Meg and Mike for a celebratory dinner, and they were all thrilled with Jimmy's gushing report about his experience. When the teacher asked who wanted to tell about their summer vacations, Jimmy had said the best part of summer for him would be this weekend at his family's picnic, and he asked if he could tell everybody about it next week.

After dinner Meg, Mo, and Mike ran through their checklists of assignments, and all were happy to report there were no complications. Mike and Jimmy were going to pick up Meg and get to the picnic site Meg had selected by nine o'clock to be sure it wasn't pre-empted by another group. They would also reserve tables by dressing them with place settings and condiments and claim a nearby grill or two for their use. Mo would arrive about eleven-thirty after stopping at Knight's Orchard in Guilford to pick up fresh corn at the popular farmers' market near Guilford's beautiful town green.

"I'll be bringing out just a couple of six packs," Mike said, "and a few bottles of white wine. Do you think that will be okay?"

"I guess so," Meg said, doing a quick head count on her fingers. "Seems like a lot though. There's only going to be six adults, right?"

"Well yeah, as invited guests. But add the three of us, that's nine, and Mary told me the Dickinsons asked if they could come. So that makes twelve when you add Stan Senior, Martha, and Stan Junior."

"That seems a little nervy, doesn't it?" Meg instantly thought her spontaneous observation was out of line and blushed, but Mike saved her from embarrassment.

"You're right. Typical of them, too. Mary called just yesterday, and I frankly was mortified I hadn't even thought about them. I bet if I had specifically asked her to invite them they wouldn't have wanted to come.

"So what do you think? Twelve adults, and I bet every one of them will drink something except Fran. Maybe even Carmen and Regina will have a beer or some wine. And lots of soda for Barbara and Martha and Jimmy. And even me!"

"I don't like the feeling I get when I'm out in the sun having wine, so you can count me out," said Meg. "What about you, Mom?"

"Oh, I kind of *like* the feeling I get," said Mo, "so you can count on me for some wine."

"I won't have more than one beer," said Mike. "I promised myself I'm going to make a good impression and not risk being a fool anymore. And I definitely don't need any more lectures from my in-laws."

"I want to make a good impression too, Mike," said Meg. "I'm as nervous as Cinderella must have been the day before the prince's ball."

"How come?" asked Mo.

"I'm just nervous about gossip, that's all. I mean there's an obvious reason for you to be there, to keep an eye on Jimmy, but what's my excuse? To keep my eye on Mike?"

They all laughed at that and Mike said, "My sister knows, the Jimmy connection aside, that you're both good friends of mine and have been for a long time. And I told Fran the same thing a couple of weeks ago."

"She asked?" Meg was surprised.

"Yeah, she asked, and that's what I told her. I said that the three of us, and Marie, have been friends for years, and the two of you have helped me and Jimmy get over some rough spots in the past four months."

"Well, I just hope Monday doesn't turn into another rough spot," said Meg. And they all agreed.

CHAPTER SEVENTEEN

It was one of the year's ten best days, and when they arrived at the Hammonassett Beach the sun was high and bright in a cloudless sky. There was a gentle, on-shore breeze from the southwest, and the air was dry. The site they had selected was perfect, and all the relatives and in-laws were there within minutes of noon, just after Mo arrived with the corn.

Introductions of Mo and Meg went easily since they stayed together, and Jimmy stuck with them. Jimmy would exclaim greetings as each guest arrived so they were drawn to him, in turns, as he introduced them to Mo and Meg. In some cases Jimmy couldn't recall more than his pet name (Papa Stan, for instance), and Stanhope Dickinson Senior would pronounce his own name and his wife's. All were cordial, and Mike was happy and relaxed as he lit the charcoal fire.

His mother and father, Michael and Gail, made their usual fuss over Jimmy and, considering their silence for the past many weeks, a nearly equal fuss over him. His father popped two beers in a row and quickly began punctuating everything he said with a blustery, usually unnecessary, chortle. Along with Tom Dickinson, he helped Mike grill the burgers and hot dogs. Gail and her mother-in-law, Martha Dickinson, at first fawned over Jimmy and then peppered Mo and Meg with questions.

"Does he have enough clothes? What does he eat? Is he sleeping well? Has he started Kindergarten? Do they go to church? Really, how *is* Mike doing? You work at Channel 5 don't you? And what do you do there, Meg? Oh, you work with Mike? Hmmm, I see."

Mary set out the tossed salads she had brought, and Mo took charge of boiling the corn over a second grill, which Mike had fired up. Meg was happy to see Carmen and Regina Torelli, now in their early twenties, and the Dickinson daughters, Barbara and Martha, with their half-child, adolescent sweetness, happily entertaining Jimmy.

"Well, you seem to be the hostess here. I wonder if you could tell me where these should go." Meg looked up from the watermelon she was slicing to see Fran holding a tray with two serving dishes of pasta salads she had agreed to bring. "I'm Jimmy's grandmother on his mother's side, Fran Torelli."

Meg was startled by this, because they had been introduced when the Torellis arrived, and she assumed Fran would realize Meg knew of the connection. But she said, "Yes, Mrs. Torelli. I know. Jimmy loves you so much, and I'm happy to finally meet you."

"Finally?" Fran arched her brows and seemed to challenge Meg with her tone of voice.

"Well of course. Jimmy's so fond of his Maman and Papa. And Carmen and Regina, too. It's a pleasure to meet you."

"He's more than fond of us," Fran abruptly retorted. "He loves us just as he still loves his dear mother. And he misses us just like he misses her. We never get to visit with him anymore. I see that's not a problem for you, though."

Mike and a few others overheard this strange outburst and he moved toward the table as Meg, blushing violently, stiffened and took a step back and away from Fran. She looked like she was about to break into tears.

"Fran. Fran," Mike said. "What's all this? You get to see Jimmy. Please don't do this now."

It seemed Fran had been preparing for a confrontation of some kind and, when her bait wasn't accepted, she suddenly deflated and walked away from Mike and Meg toward the swings where her daughters had taken Jimmy.

Meg looked sadly up at Mike, her eyes misting, and shook her head. "I knew I shouldn't have been included in this, Mike. I knew it."

"You're part of this, Meg; you belong here. Maybe it's Fran who shouldn't be here. I'm sorry. I wish I knew what it really is with her."

There were nervous glances in their direction for a moment until Stan Dickinson casually strolled up and said, "You're right, Mike. At one time or another, my brother and I and Mary have wondered about her...I don't know...attitude? Whatever, she's troubled, and it seems she always has a chip on her shoulder no matter who or what it is. Let it go." Then he gave Meg's hand a gentle squeeze and said, "Don't give it another thought, Meg. There's certainly nothing you've done. I think it's wonderful how Mo has helped Jimmy cope. And I think a lot of credit goes to you, too. Hmmm. Sorry for the speech."

Stan's unexpected and gratuitous familiarity with Meg, despite his seemingly well-intentioned gesture, jolted Mike into recalling the proposition, drunk or not, that Stan forced on Marie at their engagement party, and he bristled. Pulling Meg back to his side, Mike said, "Right, Stan. We don't need the speech; Fran does—and probably attention, too. Let's check the hamburgers, Meg," and he whispered to her that he would explain about Stan later.

As Mike steered Meg away from a silenced Stan, Stan's dad and brother were bringing a full platter of hamburgers and hot dogs from the grill, and Mike broke the tension by calling out, "Let's eat, everybody."

The next hour or two seemed like old times for the three families, with lots of conversation, jokes, and stories going back over the years to the days of Mike and Marie's engagement. Jimmy romped from one small group to another, amusing everyone and being amused. Mike enjoyed his one beer and saw he was correct about the general consumption level.

And he took a lot of pleasure in all the reminiscences.

Meg seemed to have recovered from the shock of Fran's rude confrontation, and she brought around the serving dishes, encouraging everyone to second helpings. Fran was frosty; though whether from embarrassment or venom it was hard to tell. Mary, Gail, and the rest of the Dickinsons weren't making any effort to engage the Torellis in casual conversation, however, and Mike again reflected on the depth of their apparent prejudices. He was happy though, to see that Carmen and Regina were comfortable with Barbara and Martha, and he hoped that was more than just the younger girls looking up to their slightly older counterparts. The only one above it all, except for Jimmy, was Mo, who was obviously relishing the mix of people and food and engaging in interesting and relaxed conversation with everyone.

Not long after the leftovers were packed up, the paper plates and plastic forks and cups bagged for trash and the last watermelon slices quickly disappearing, Mike looked around and realized Meg was gone. Frowning, he caught Mo's eye and mouthed, "Where's Meg?" He hoped she'd gone to the restrooms but he feared the worst, and he was right. Mo gestured toward the second grill, which had been used to cook the corn, and when she and Mike met there she said, "Meg had to leave, Mike. I gave her my car."

"For God's sake, Mo, is she sick?"

"She's upset, Mike. It will pass; there was just too much going on here...the tension, Fran's nonsense, all the old stories. She'll be okay."

"She was right," Mike said. "I was wrong. What a mess."

"No one ever knows what will happen when in-laws are thrown together," Mo counseled. "Guess what? Jimmy had a great time; and so did I. And apparently it was 'business as usual' with Fran. I could tell no one was really shocked by her rudeness. Hey, life goes on."

She's right, Mike thought. *No one ever knows. And it was a remarkably good day for the others.* But he felt terribly about Meg.

"She'll be at my place, Mike. You can drive me home and pick up

Meg. All she'll miss is helping with the trash."

At that moment, Jimmy ran up to them. "Where did Meg go, Daddy? Did she leave?"

"Yes, Jimmy. She wasn't feeling well. You and I will pick her up at Aunt Mo's."

Suddenly, from a nearby table they heard Fran point out to no one in particular, "Well I guess I should feel better he isn't calling her 'Mommy' already." Conversations hushed as everyone turned to stare in her direction.

The shocked silence was chilling until Jimmy said, "My mommy's dead now, Maman. But we had fun, didn't we?" Fran reddened visibly and thrust out her chin but said nothing. Thomas looked away from her in embarrassment.

Mike leaned to lift Jimmy into his arms and a bear hug. "We all had fun, Jimmy. And Mommy would have had the most fun." To the others who were quietly watching, he said, "Well I guess it's time to go, everybody. Thanks for coming and for all your good food." He let Jimmy down to help Mo gather up the remaining plates and soft drink cans and walked over to say goodbye to his parents and the Dickinsons.

He was angry with Fran—as angry as he could be—and decided to ignore her and Thomas as he, Jimmy, and Mo left the park. When they turned to go he could see Thomas engaged in a quiet but vehement conversation with his wife, who was shaking her head and, it seemed, beginning to cry.

"Look, Fran," Thomas said to his wife, "it's time to move ahead. I know it's been only four months, and sure your feelings are hurt, but we both have to do better. We can't let jealousy take us now; for Jimmy's sake, for our peace, for everyone. Just stop. Please just stop, Fran."

* * * * *

Meg was happily finishing up the preparation of two lasagnas she'd decided would be easy for dinner (a small one for Mo, and the other for

Mike and Jimmy) when the three of them arrived at Mo's apartment. Mike was relieved with her bright-eyed, welcoming smile.

"We missed you," Mike said. "But I sure understand why you left, and I feel terrible about upsetting you. Fran's a little crazy it seems."

"It's okay, Mike. I've been thinking about it, and it's really not as big a deal as I felt it was in the park. 'Baptism by fire,' I guess, and you're right, that was crazy behavior. It was a fun time anyway, right, Jimmy?"

"Yup," Jimmy agreed. "What are you making?"

"Dinner for you and Aunt Mo. Lasagna's your favorite."

"I knew it. Goody! Thanks, Meg. But if we're taking you home, why don't we have the lasagna there? Or at our place?"

They ended up at Mike and Jimmy's apartment, and after Jimmy went to bed, Meg and Mike sat at the kitchen table and sorted through the day's events.

Mike was impressed with Meg's resilience; he probably would have fussed and fumed for days if he had been the butt of such unmannerly treatment. And he was happy that everyone else seemed to welcome Meg's presence as much as they understood Mo's, and welcomed her, too. "I'm sure my 'normal' relatives think you and your mom are pretty normal, yourselves. And I guess we can see what Fran has been struggling with. That's a bit of a relief. So it wasn't such a bad idea after all, right?"

"It was a great idea, Mike. You heard Jimmy agree. You did a great job. And, I think, a great favor for the families and for Jimmy. Pulling them together. They loved it."

"You really get the credit for pulling it off, Meg. Only the idea was mine. Your planning made it work. Thank you."

Meg blushed and bowed her head, and Mike reached over and, cupping her cheeks with his hands, raised her head so she was looking right at him. "They loved it, Meg. And I love you. Don't say anything. Put your arms around my shoulders. Is it okay if I kiss you?"

"Oh yes, Mike. Oh yes." And Meg kissed him back as gently as Mike had kissed her. And then more intensely as his arms encircled her—and more urgently.

"Do you think it's okay if you spend the night?" Mike asked. "With me?"

"Oh yes, Mike. Please kiss me some more."

For each of them it was, at once, like the very first time they had ever kissed someone romantically...in the sixth grade or seventh grade. Tentative at first; lips barely touching; breathing softly; lips gliding across cheeks and noses; lips caressing eyelids, eyebrows, ears, earlobes, foreheads. Exploring. Relaxing. Shoulders, arms, torsos— yielding; sinking against each other's.

Mike slipped off his chair, to his knees, pulling Meg closer to him, and she let herself be pulled, his face dropping from her face to her chest, and she pulled his head to her breasts. Then she slipped off her own chair to meet Mike, knee-to-knee on the linoleum floor of his kitchen, locked in an unbalanced embrace that their knees weren't used to.

"Meg?" Mike whispered.

"Yes?" she answered.

"Meg, there's a thing you should know," he said.

Gasping, "What, Mike?" she asked.

Then Mike in his Irish brogue said, "On your knees on the kitchen floor is no place for a fine lass like yourself. You'll be getting yourself up and into that bedroom before the help sees ya, or my name isn't Mike Flynn. D'ye hear me now?"

Meg burst into laughter, and wantonly shook her breasts at him as she leaped to her feet, pulled him up, and said, "I'll race you."

CHAPTER EIGHTEEN

As the temperature edged cooler over the next few weeks, there was an obvious lift in Mike's stride, personality, and energy–in everything he did. Mo caught it immediately and had known at once when she saw Meg's glow at lunch, the day after the picnic, that romance had taken charge! Even Mo felt more energetic; hummed a favorite tune more often, said hello to other residents whom she'd never met, and began daydreaming about wedding bells.

Jimmy reported on his family picnic as he had promised, the day after the picnic, and delighted his classmates with little seashells he had collected for them from the Hammonasset beach.

"Best was, I learned all their names, Aunt Mo," Jimmy said, "because Mrs. Meyer asked them to write thank you notes to me."

"Really," said Mo. "Can they all write that well, Jimmy?"

"Oh no, Aunt Mo. They all made drawings, but most could write their names. So I remembered them."

September flew by with Jimmy reporting daily on more and more adventures in school. Mrs. Meyer called everything an adventure, and the Kindergartners believed it from the very first day. Every Friday they would be assigned a "weekend adventure," and they never thought that reporting on the best thing that happened to them was, in reality, homework.

Mary called a few days after the picnic to thank Mike ("and please tell Meg, too") for hosting the picnic. "Is Meg okay, Mike? I mean she disappeared so quickly after, well..."

"After Fran behaved like trash," Mike finished. "Yes, Meg is fine, Mary, and I've explained to her what is really troubling Fran. Thomas surprised me when he took her down a couple of pegs before we left, and it's clear he knows right from wrong. Remember, Fran and Thomas promised to take care of Jimmy and then slapped me in the face with their broken promise. And now they want to slap around one of the sweetest women they'll ever meet. Well maybe not Thomas, but...well, Fran will heal in time, I hope."

"Mike, are you that naïve?" Mary asked. "The Torellis have problems with the Irish; just as our dad had problems with the Italians. But Dad was smacked into better behavior by Mom's protestant-neutral insistence that he rid himself of inbred prejudices. And you would have never felt any of this if Marie had survived. Forget it. Fran just can't help herself no matter how hard that sweet Thomas tries to help her."

"I guess that's part of it, honey," Mike said to his sister. "But I think I understand Fran, and it's hard. Thomas and Fran Torelli are my parents-in-law, and I don't want them getting down on me for what really is their problem. Let's give her time."

"I'll work on it, Mike, but meanwhile look at what Meg has done for you. Why do you think I'm spending so much time on the phone right now? Because I love working through things with you when you're alert and responsive and..."

"Sober?" Mike said

"That's right. You were so fine at the picnic and in control; like the old days. We were so proud of you. We love you, Mike."

"I know Mary. I know you love me. And Jimmy and I love you too, just as Marie did."

"Thanks, Mike. That's so good to hear." Jumping tracks, Mary said,

"What do you think about you, Jimmy, Meg, Mo, and all the Torellis joining us for Thanksgiving this year? It's a couple of months away, plenty of time for a thaw between Fran and the rest of us, and it would be a good way to rebuild bridges."

"That's awfully generous, Mary. You know Fran certainly won't take the first step. Are you sure?"

"Absolutely," Mary said. "Best part is we could all be with Stanhope and Martha in Simsbury. That's really neutral ground and ought to keep everyone at their best. They would really love it if Meg and I coordinated the whole thing. What do you say?"

"I hope it happens, Mary. Thanks. I'm seeing Meg tomorrow night for dinner at Mo's, and I'll tell them. Jimmy will be all excited over another family party so soon. Meg will call you."

Meg was at first taken aback in thinking about tempting the Torellis to another clash, but she quickly realized this wasn't a problem of hers. Mike and Mary and the others had the problem; she was interested in what was best for Jimmy and, of course, Mike and her.

So, in the morning Meg called Mary from Channel 5, and they met to make plans a few weeks later, on a Saturday toward the end of September, at a fun restaurant, The Solo, in Farmington. They split the calling list and, to be sensitive, agreed that Mary would call the Torellis and Meg would call Carmen and Regina. At the time this seemed to make the most sense since Meg was just a few years older than the Torelli sisters, and there was some nice chemistry among the three of them.

With the multi-family camaraderie renewed at the "Hamonnasett Picnic," there were immediate commitments to the event, except from Fran and Thomas. Mary had left three phone messages, and these hadn't been returned despite ready acceptances from Carmen and Regina.

Mary called Meg to report this and they agreed to just let it go in the hopes Thomas and, particularly, Fran would come around and accept. Meg and Mike wondered, though, and although they asked each other, "Is this thing really that bad?" they certainly felt that it wasn't that good.

So the plans were coming together, and there were lots of strong family opinions as calls went back and forth about the appetizers, side dishes, and desserts.

This marked a renewal of family regard and affection for each other, which had seemed to drain away in the months Marie had become ill, declined, and died. Joy was back in the air, but no one wanted to ask, "What about Fran?" And it wasn't "Fran and Thomas." It was Fran.

Jimmy reported that the new adventure in Kindergarten was Mrs. Meyer's suggestion to her class that each of them work on a Paper Mache centerpiece for Thanksgiving dinner.

"What a fine adventure, Jimmy," Mo said. "What are you going to make?"

Jimmy told her that most of his classmates were making turkeys, which is what Mo expected he would be doing, but no. "I'm making a Pilgrim," Jimmy said.

"Oh what fun, Jimmy." Mo was thinking about his ability to extend his notion of the holiday way beyond the traditional dinner accompaniments and into the origins of the holiday feast. "But that sounds like a pretty complicated Paper Mache, Jimmy. Won't a Pilgrim involve a lot of arms and legs? Sounds hard to me."

"Well maybe, Aunt Mo, but I'm making a lady Pilgrim—as pretty as I can, like Mommy and you and Meg. And she's going to be so easy to make, because she will have a big round skirt, like your Aunt Jemima cookie jar, and she'll be holding a turkey on a tray in front of her. So it's really easy except for her head, but I'm going to put a bonnet on her, so no ears."

Mo was inwardly convulsed with the humor in all of this, particularly using her Aunt Jemima cookie jar, but equally impressed with his idea. She clapped her hands saying, "Jimmy, you are so clever. What did Mrs. Meyer think?"

"That's hard to tell," Jimmy said. "She looked away from me for a minute, and when she turned around she was all smiley but with tears. I guess she had a sad thought. Anyway, she said that would be great. You know the best part? She said if I had time I should do an Indian lady. Same way, except with a tray of corn and a feather in her hair."

CHAPTER NINETEEN

Now late October with Thanksgiving just four weeks away, there had been no response from the Torellis. Meg had mentioned this to Carmen and Regina, and they seemed to be as puzzled as everyone else.

"Are they okay?" Mike asked when Meg told him what she had learned.

Meg said, "Well of course. The girls would have told us. I think they're just ashamed."

"What's hard," Mike said, "is that you have been so good, so loving. None of this should be going on, but I'm trying to understand."

Meg's shoulders started to heave and she turned away from him and then started to sob and sob.

"Oh honey. Honey. You *are* so good. You *are* so loving. Please don't. Please. I love you. Jimmy loves you. We couldn't live without you." And he put his arms around her and, standing, rocked side to side, nuzzling her neck until she stopped, turned, embraced, and kissed him.

A couple of days later Stan Dickinson the junior called Meg at home to say how much his folks were looking forward to Thanksgiving in Simsbury, as was he. Meg was gracious, cordial, and curious about his call to her since his sister-in-law, Mary, was the contact for his invitation.

Ever the party gal though, Meg attempted a move to figure this out and said, "Wonderful, Stan. Mary told me; how wonderful of your folks to open their home to all of us."

"Oh sure, Meg. It's all family. They love this stuff. Well, mostly all family. I mean, you know, the Torellis. But yeah, this will be great."

"So," Meg asked, "you called to tell me what your appetizer or dessert or favorite wine is that you'll be bringing, right?"

Side-stepping that, Stan said, "You know, Meg, I really called to thank you for all you've done in being the glue that's brought our families back together. And not just since Marie died; we've been slowly drifting apart since the wedding."

Meg had no idea what to say next except, "Well thanks, Stan. And thanks for calling."

She was about to ring off when Stan said, "Right. Of course. You're welcome. But I called to invite you to visit my store in Farmington. We all know how much your mom has done to help Mike and Jimmy through all this, and I'm inviting you to find something Mo would like for Christmas... at a deep discount that only family members get."

"How lovely, Stan. What a lovely thought, but I don't know." Meg asked herself, *Whatever is he thinking about?* "Mo and I aren't really family, Stan. Close like a family, yes, but I'm really sensitive to raising any more eyebrows."

"Oh. Well, I hope you're not right about that," Stan said, "but think about it, and maybe you'll have second thoughts by Thanksgiving. I hope so."

Later, Meg wondered if Stan was fishing for something. Or flirting. Or brazenly making a pass. But she was on her way to see Mike and Jimmy and concluded he probably was just being terribly nice, and she set it aside.

On the short drive, she chuckled over Jimmy's Thanksgiving project, which Mo had called her about earlier. And when she arrived she let Jimmy tell her himself, and she piled on even more compliments while making a mental note to ensure Mary's Thanksgiving table would be able to accommodate the two Paper Mache figures.

In the few weeks leading up to the holiday party, Jimmy continued to excel in school, loved his adventures, and brought home interesting reports every day. Mike was happily back at work, and there seemed to be considerably more respect among his colleagues for him as a parent-manager, good dad, and competent salesman able to roll with the punches and land on his feet. He and Meg took lunch together just once a week to avoid encouraging the rumor mill, which was always anxious for more gossip. And Meg's job was, as she said, "more fun than ever."

While The Beanery served up a tasty array of good food ("odd, but healthy" was what Mike called it), Meg was eager to get back to Phelan's so Mike could catch up with his pals; she was so proud of his easy ability to be comfortable with coffee or Diet Coke or tonic water. All his pals were happy to see him, and Tim Halloran continued to pelt him with beer coasters.

So the fall days passed easily and comfortably, and the Torellis finally called to confirm their attendance for Thanksgiving. Meg learned from Carmen and Regina that Thomas had experienced a sudden spike in his PSA test for prostate trouble and had withdrawn, in misery and anxiety, for a month.

It made a lot of sense that Fran, legendary for drawing attention to herself, would have relished getting the word out and basking in the empathy-sympathy "tsk-tsks," flowers and, perhaps, a special sainthood for being such a loving, caring wife.

So while all were concerned about Thomas, they were pleasantly surprised that Fran may have reined in her usual selfish behavior. Everyone, of course, was relieved that the Thanksgiving invitation had been accepted, thus putting some closure on the Hammonasset incident.

A few days later Meg brought up Stan's call to her and told Mike she first felt confused but at the end thought he was making an innocent gesture as she might expect if she were a real family member. "Maybe he was sort of letting me know that Mo and I were considered part of the Flynn/Dickinson/Torelli families. Maybe he wanted me, us really, to know that despite the Torelli mystery, everything was going the way we'd like it to be. I did feel good about that, Mike."

"Well I don't feel very good about Stan's call. Not good at all. Do you know of anyone else who would make an out-of-the-blue offer like that? I mean, particularly over the phone. In person at a party maybe, but over the phone? What else did he say?"

"That's all," Meg said. "About me being the glue and Mom's support for you and Jimmy. What I told you. I really wasn't uncomfortable, just surprised I guess. And I really think I was flattered that he would offer a family discount in his antique shop."

"Well I'm more suspicious than you, Meg, and jealous, and mainly protective. And I'll tell you why."

Meg's eyes widened, and she gasped as Mike told her about Stan propositioning Marie at their engagement party. "You know, Meg, Marie was so tough and big-hearted she just held it in until after we were married, God love her. But once is enough. And I mean it."

"If he calls you again though, I want to know right away. I'll call back and let him know that we're thinking about his offer. I'll also tell him that I know about the pass he made at Marie at our engagement party and that I won't stand for anything like that again. So let's do it that way."

* * * * *

The following week, Meg got a nice promotion, still supervising the Channel 5 traffic department (now with three people there, including herself), but also managing schedules for syndicated broadcast activity and spot ad placement within network television programming.

She told Mike while on their way to Mo's for dinner, and Mike could tell from her rosy glow that this was really big news. So he grinned and played dumb by asking, "What does all that mean, Meg?"

She laughed and said, "Lots of opportunity for you to make more money, which you won't, by the way, if you let anyone know that you don't know what it means."

"Oh yeah? If we weren't on the way to your mom's right now, I'd pull this car over and let you find out how much I know about things...sex, for instance."

Meg shrieked and said, "Go ahead, I dare you," and when Mike swerved over two lanes to exit at the Long Wharf Shopping Mall along the harbor shoreline, she shrieked again and said, "No, you can't. My mother will know in a second. Besides, Jimmy will be there."

"Oh really? Well we better make this fast then. By the way, how will your mother know?"

"She always knows what's up when you walk in with that la-la-land, goofy grin on your face. Anyone would know."

Mike pretended to bawl his unhappiness as he re-entered traffic for another quarter mile to the exit for Mo's place, and Meg leaned over and gave his cheek a big kiss saying, "Any other time, soldier."

Jimmy met them at the door to Mo's, all excited, and rushed them into the small dining room where Mo had set out a beautiful Irish linen table cloth on which Jimmy's Paper Mache Pilgrim and Indian ladies took center stage. To set them off, they were surrounded by some colorful Maple leaves Mo and Jimmy had gathered up from the grounds outside, and the effect was stunning.

Meg was the first to react, "Oh Jimmy, they are wonderful—just beautiful. What a lovely adventure you've been on. Give me a hug."

And Jimmy jumped into her outstretched arms as Mike said, "Good for you, Jimmy. Great job."

"Next year, Daddy, I'm going to make a Mr. Pilgrim and Mr. Indian. Do you think Aunt Mary's table will be big enough?" And they all laughed and agreed that the Dickinsons would find plenty of room for the Pilgrims and Indians.

It was a Friday night, and after a lasagna dinner together Mo, Meg, and Mike stayed at the table while Jimmy watched a movie Mo had rented for him on their way home from school. Mary had called Meg earlier in the day to confirm their Thanksgiving plans, and Meg shared that news with

Mo and Mike. Then she said, "I meant to tell you this on the way here from work, Mike, but we were a bit distracted." Mike grinned, and it was obvious Mo caught on at once when she said, "Can't the two of you behave?"

"Mary said Carmen told her Fran and Thomas had changed their minds and wouldn't be with us next week after all. She said that her dad was upset, and they thought they'd spoil our fun. What we can't figure out is why Fran–or even Thomas–hadn't called Mary. It's really hard to make sense of it, but Mary seems relieved. A bit insulted maybe, but her tension is gone.

"Well then it's for the best," Mo said. "Too bad but better for everyone."

And Mo was right. They all had a great day. Carmen and Regina were wonderful helpers, and Fran had sent along with them her candied yams, which seemed to mean that everything was okay; no problem. All agreed the yams were certainly fine. Jimmy's Pilgrim and Indian ladies stole the show, and he promised to make husbands for the ladies next year. Mike had just two glasses of wine and was charming, with some good jokes requiring his Irish brogue for full effect.

Meg and Mary were delighted with their co-hosting in the senior Stanhope's home, and Stan Junior busied himself, bringing wood in from the porch and maintaining the fires in both the living and dining rooms.

Meg had been apprehensive about Stan, perhaps repeating his invitation to visit the store, but all he said at the end of the day was, "Don't forget my offer, Meg."

Mike was with Meg when this happened and asked Meg later if that was Stan's only reference. "That was it, Mike. I guess he really was being thoughtful and generous."

It was quiet for a moment; then Mike said, "Stan better not mention that again."

CHAPTER TWENTY

Jimmy became increasingly excited as the next few weeks flew toward Christmas. The Christmas Tree Lighting Ceremony on the New Haven Green dazzled him. Multiple sightings of Santa Claus served to confirm what he knew about Santa's helpers. His visit with the "real" Santa at the mall convinced him, because, "He knew my name, Daddy!"

In an early letter, Jimmy asked Santa if his presents could be left at Aunt Mo's, and to his delight Santa agreed he'd be doing that.

Oddly, Carmen and Regina had been unable to baby-sit since Thanksgiving, but all decided it wasn't worth making anything of it. Coincidental, they hoped.

A few days before Christmas, Meg, Mike, and Jimmy were at Mo's for dinner and, after the table was cleared, had fun wrapping Christmas gifts. Jimmy took turns helping first Mike, then Meg with their bows, ribbons, and tape. Mo and Jimmy went to the guest room to work on his out of sight.

Mo served a big pitcher of eggnog laced with rum for a treat; Jimmy had his own eggnog, "straight," and he thought it was an ice cream soda it was so tasty.

"A package arrived here yesterday for you, Meg, from Stan's antique shop," Mo said. "The label reads, 'Open Me before Christmas!'"

"For Meg?" Mike looked up in surprise. "What's that all about?"

"Well it's really addressed to Meg and Jimmy," Mo said. "Let's see what it is."

Mike looked at Meg and said, "Yeah, let's see what Stan's up to. The nerve of that guy. Anyone want another eggnog?"

As Mike took his mug out to the kitchen, Meg and Jimmy opened Stan's gift to find a first edition printing of Clement Moore's famous poem, "A Visit from St. Nicholas." The ladies squealed with surprise and delight over the unexpected treasure, and Jimmy asked, "What is it, Aunt Mo? What is it, Meg?"

Mike said, "Yeah, what is it, Meg?" mimicking Jimmy. "What's the big deal with Stan's gift to you and Jimmy?" Then he poured another shot of rum into his eggnog before returning from the kitchen.

The women quickly glanced at each other, alarm evident in their eyes—an exchange that Mike caught. "And what's the big deal with another delicious eggnog for me? Come on, it's Christmas, and I've been one of Santa's good little boys. Not like Uncle Stan. Right, Jimmy?"

Mike had reached the dining table and slid into his chair next to Jimmy, whom he pulled close to him with a hug and a kiss on Jimmy's brow. "Right, Jimmy?"

Eyes wide with puzzlement, Jimmy said, "I don't know, Daddy. Show me his book, Aunt Mo. What is it?"

Mo said, "Let's go into the living room, Jimmy. Aunt Mo will show you the book. It's a poem I first remember hearing when I was just about your age. I'll read it to you." And Mo gently pulled Jimmy away from the table into the other room.

"Hey, Mo," Mike called after her, "I can read that to Jimmy. Come on."

"Mike," Meg said, "please stay here with me. Mo and Jimmy will be fine. I just want a minute to..." and she started to softly cry.

"Hey, Meg, this isn't my fault. Stan started this whole mess. He thinks he can step in front of me like he tried to do with Marie, and this time to send a big shot book to my son and you? And he still wants to send stuff to Mo? What's that all about? And you and Mo think that's okay? Well it's not, and I told you I would call him if he tried anything funny, and I'm doing that right now."

Mike stood and lurched to the kitchen for the wireless phone, and Meg started after him. "Mike. Don't call Stan. Please, Mike. I really think you've had more eggnog than you realize. This would not be a good time to call. Let's do that tomorrow."

"Oh. So this is a bad time for me, but a good time for Stan to step in and mess with you and Jimmy and Mo, and I just let him do it?" Mike reached for the rum, and Meg didn't know whether to be relieved or not to see there was barely a tablespoon left in the bottle. *Where did it all go?* she wondered, glad that the rum was gone but worried about how far gone Mike was.

"Mike. You've been so good. Please stop. Forget the book; forget Stan. I don't care what he does. I care about you...and Jimmy. And now I'm worried about you and Jimmy getting home safely."

"You don't have to worry about Jimmy and me, Meg. We're okay. You should worry about you...and Stan. That worries me. That really makes me worry. Jimmy and I will get home okay. We have to go."

"Daddy! You have to hear this poem. There's a real Santa Claus, and he can do all sorts of things. Just like you, Daddy."

Mo was right behind Jimmy as he ran to his dad in the kitchen. Mike scooped him up, and Meg shrugged at her mom and let her eyes wander to the ceiling to indicate she had no idea what the next move should be.

"Ah Jimmy. Me boyo," Mike said in his brogue. "I love ya, Jimmy, and wish yer mom was here to see what a fine lad you've turned out to be." Mike put Jimmy down and said, "Let me look at ya. A fine lad, indeed. Give me a hug now." As Jimmy ran into his dad's outstretched arms, his momentum, slight as it was, pushed Mike back and into an open cabinet door, which struck Mike right on his temple, and he slid in a heap to the floor.

"Daddy! Daddy!" screamed Jimmy. "Oh, Daddy, wake up. I'm sorry, Daddy."

Fortunately, Mike wasn't knocked out—just a bit loopy—and despite his several, rum-laced eggnogs, was able to roll up onto an elbow and project a goofy and somewhat crooked grin at the trio of highly concerned faces staring down at him. "Ya look like you're at a wake I think, and I'm the one you're waking. What's going on here?"

"Oh, Daddy! You're okay," Jimmy said. "You scared us. Please get up, Daddy. Want some water?"

"Water is just what I want, Jimmy. A tall glass with lots of ice. And then a cup of coffee. Could you fix that for me, Mo? And you, Meg... thanks. This is the wrong thing for you—for us. How do I get this way? Please help me. I love you." And Mike started to tremble, and tears came to his eyes. Meg knelt next to him and gathered him into her arms.

After a few minutes, an abashed Mike excused himself to take a calming, lukewarm shower. While he was out of the room, Meg told her mother about Stan and Marie and Mike's determination to protect her from Stan... imagined, innocent, meaningless—it didn't matter.

CHAPTER TWENTY-ONE

Mike was so upset with himself in the morning—remorseful even, that he was convinced he was beyond help. "I've read the articles about alcoholics," he muttered to himself. "I know about the guilt, the paranoia...look at the hold Stan's behavior has on me...now falling down on the floor in front of Jimmy. Really wasn't his push; it was me losing my balance. Like a wino falling off a bench on The Green."

After more coffee the night before, Meg had driven behind Jimmy and Mike back to their apartment. Jimmy had dozed off as Mo finished reading to him, and the accidental tumble seemed to have shocked Mike back to sobriety. Mike had been contrite, and Mo and Meg had to just let it go.

After Mike had tucked Jimmy in, he and Meg had sat quietly for a few minutes, both relieved that this episode was done with. Finally Mike said, "Good thing we hadn't planned to go to the station party tomorrow, huh?" And he grinned.

Meg laughed at the droll way he was able to warm up a chilly situation and, more importantly, not lug around the guilt he must have felt. Her dad relied on guilt, and that used to drive her and Mo crazy. So it was easy for both of them to kiss goodnight and agree to meet for morning coffee at work.

As he drove Jimmy to Mo's, his son couldn't wait to hear more about Donner and Blitzen. And when he got there, Mike stammered more apologies to Mo. He really was at a loss for a rational explanation.

"We'll all have to work through this, Mike," said Mo. "I've got to be more careful; as careful as you have been. Meg and I have been through the 'enabling' stuff, and we know there's no laughing it off. And with you there's a lot more involved that will help you win. You've got all this love and hope and future ahead of you—with Jimmy and Meg." Then she chuckled and broke a huge smile, "And I hope, with me as a mother-in-law!"

It was all Mike could do to hold back his tears as he stepped forward and pulled Mo to him saying, "Thank you, Mo. That's the way it's going to be. Thank you."

* * * * * *

At work, Channel 5 was alive with festive spirit and twinkling decorations; a dusting of snow was covering the ground with the thin but white carpet Jimmy had been looking forward to, for Santa's sake, for weeks, and Meg and Mike enjoyed the intimacy of their coffee conversation, the way it always is for lovers, then split up to clear their desks and firm up schedules for the long, holiday weekend.

Since Christmas was on a Saturday this year, the station was allowing a day off on Friday, Christmas Eve, to enable an extended, holiday weekend. And the Flynns and Donlons had made big plans for themselves. The rest of their extended families would get phone calls of Christmas cheer, but these next three days were to be spent among just the four of them, beginning Friday morning for shopping, buying their tree, and going to the Christmas Eve Vigil Mass at five o'clock.

Only four blocks from Mo's apartment was a corner parking lot where Christmas trees were sold and now, the day before Christmas Eve morning, just nine or ten were left when Meg and Mo and Jimmy and Mike met there at eleven o'clock.

As you'd expect, choices included some very tall and skinny trees and some fairly short and stubby ones. The four of them were the only customers and the cheerful, pipe-smoking vendor was the head custodian in Mo's building and knew her and Meg well—and had for years.

"Wondered when you would finally get here, Mo," Charlie said. "I have my six best trees hidden under that tarp, and my other best customers might have beaten you to them. How about some hot chocolate?"

This unexpected treat caused Jimmy's eyes to enlarge like the Star of Bethlehem, and he and Charlie shook hands as he was given his cup.

Mike and Meg toured the leftovers on display in the lot, just to be sure, while Charlie dusted the new, one-inch cover of clean snow off the tarp. Mo always wondered if Charlie counted everyone among his best customers and kept re-stocking the choices he had hidden. So she was mightily impressed seeing that the snow covering the tarp was undisturbed.

Charlie pulled all six of them out and asked Jimmy, "What size do you think you'd like?"

"We need a sort of small one I think. What do you think, Aunt Mo?"

"A small one? Hmmm. I thought you would want a big tree. How come?"

"I was thinking about where our tree will go, Aunt Mo, and how much room you have."

"There's lots of room, Jimmy. Pick the one you like best."

"Well there might not be that much room," Jimmy said, "when Santa Claus leaves all our presents. So I think small; how about this one?"

The others thought Jimmy's calculation was hilarious and laughed aloud, with Charlie leading the way. "Good thinking, young man. If I were you I'd do the same thing. Suppose you take this one and put it on top of this packing crate. That way it will be almost three feet off the floor, so plenty of room for Santa but still taller than your dad."

Mo said, "And we can put our big green sheet around the crate, Jimmy. It will be beautiful!"

So all were delighted, and when Charlie had put some netting around the tree, it fit nicely in Mike's trunk with just the tip emerging.

They were back at Mo's in five minutes, had the tree up in another ten, and then took their time with the lights and balls and other ornaments for more than an hour. Mo had her long-time favorite Christmas tapes playing, and for lunch they ate Jimmy's cold-weather favorites—hot tomato soup and toasted, grilled cheese sandwiches.

After Jimmy's nap, then snack, it was time for the five o'clock vigil Mass which was an ecumenical service and children's Christmas pageant in the small chapel right on the condo grounds. Lots of singing with the local children costumed as wise men, shepherds, angels, Mary, and Joseph. A two-month-old infant appeared as baby Jesus and, astonishingly, slept straight through. Jimmy was enchanted; the Episcopal and Catholic priests grinned and blessed everyone; candles glowed, and *Silent Night* was magical.

The plan was for Meg to share her mother's room and Jimmy and Mike to sleep in the guest bedroom. After the service, they drove straight to the pizza parlor just outside the condo gate, picked up their order, then stopped to wish a Merry Christmas to Charlie and hand him two extra slices Mike had bought.

It was wonderful back at Mo's with more music, *Amahl and the Night Visitors* on television, then *A Visit from St. Nicholas* before Jimmy went to bed. Very nice. No beer, wine, whiskey, or eggnog, and lots of hugs all around.

CHAPTER TWENTY-TWO

Christmas day was lovely, with some gifts, a visit to Marie's grave to place her Christmas wreath and say some prayers, lots more. Mike and Meg learned Thomas Torelli's prostate trouble was under control; Meg called Stan and put Jimmy on the phone to thank him for *A Visit from St. Nicholas*; Meg told Stan it was all such a rush, she felt rude not to have accepted his offer. "Maybe next year?" she asked.

"Of course," said Stan.

In a private moment, Mike told Meg of Mo's hope to be his mother-in-law some day and their hug.

Meg was thrilled. "What did you say, Mike?"

"I told her that is the way it's going to be," and he leaned over and kissed her sweetly. "If that's the way you want it to be, Meg."

The week after Christmas flew by, since Friday was New Year's Eve and another day off for most people. So it was another long holiday weekend to look forward to. Mike was busy all week calling on advertisers to sell year-end inventory to make what was a record year for him even better. He even had to pass on their regular lunch together to nail down the sale of commercial time still available before the weekend.

Meg was a bit hurt by that, but they had a big date planned for a New Year's Eve gala, which they had been invited to, at Mory's, the world-famous restaurant that was home to the Yale Wiffenpoofs singing group, and they both were excited. In fact, Meg was relieved by Mike's distractions so she and Mo could put together her "knock-out" outfit for welcoming in a new year.

Jimmy had the week off and never had more fun. The "tall" small tree worked perfectly, and Santa had put so many more toys in the area that Jimmy was able to exclaim, "See, Daddy! This is the best!" So Jimmy had toys and games and new clothes galore to keep him busy. And suddenly, Carmen was available to baby-sit during Mo's shopping trips with Meg. This was great for Jimmy, and Carmen was taken aback by how much he had grown—first, since the picnic but even more in the one month since Thanksgiving.

Jimmy spent New Year's Eve at Aunt Mo's, and a good thing he did. His dad and Meg had partied the entire night long (no drinks) and came rolling into Mo's apartment at eight o'clock jokingly demanding breakfast. Mo was up, of course, and Jimmy was still in his pajamas but came tearing out of the bathroom, toothbrush still between his teeth, when he heard the commotion and laughter in the living room.

"Well! This is a fine kettle of fish," Mike said, in his brogue. "Just rolled out of bed, and breakfast not on the table, I see. And this being the start of a new year? Give me a hug my man. And don't knock me over again if yer don't mind."

That was all Jimmy needed to engage in a tickling, screaming, gasping, "I think I'm going to pee, Daddy," wrestle that lasted close to a minute—a near record.

Meg was busy hugging her mother, and then everyone switched to hug those, as-yet, un-hugged, and Meg tooted on her New Year's noise-maker and proclaimed, "Happy New Year!" which sent Mo into the kitchen to reappear with a pitcher of orange juice for a toast.

With that Mike said, "Jimmy, come with me, young man, and we'll get some proper clothes on for the New Year. Meg, could you help us find Jimmy's new Christmas sweater? Wouldn't that be nice?"

In the guest room, Meg could see that Mike was nervous. *What's wrong*, she thought. And then she realized why Mike had asked her to help, and she knelt on the rug next to Jimmy and put an arm around his waist.

Mike also knelt, facing Jimmy, and said, "I love you just as much as you love me, Jimmy. You know that. And Meg loves you at least that much. Maybe more."

"I know that too, Daddy."

"Jimmy, I've asked Meg to marry me—to be my wife. And she said yes, which means she will be your new mommy. Won't that be a dream come true?"

"Oh, Daddy. That means Meg will be with us all the time. I'm so happy." And he turned to put both arms around Meg and kiss her.

Suddenly, Jimmy looked up at his dad and asked, "Will this be okay with my first mommy, Daddy? Will she be happy?"

"Your first mommy loves us all," said Mike, "and she will be happy about anything that brings happiness to us. Remember, she will always be in our prayers."

Jimmy grinned then asked, "Does Aunt Mo know?"

"Not yet, Jimmy. Your new mommy and I thought we should all tell Aunt Mo together. What do you think?"

"Let's go, Meg...I mean Mommy...and give Aunt Mo some hugs."

Mo was setting the tray of juice glasses on the coffee table as Jimmy, Meg, and Mike came into the room. The new Christmas sweater had been forgotten, and Jimmy was still in his pajamas, but the three of them were wearing the broadest grins Mo thought she'd ever seen.

"Okay you three, what's going on?" And then she saw Meg's diamond ring. "Oh. Oh mercy. How wonderful. Oh Meg, I'm so happy for you. And for Mike and Jimmy." And they hugged. And the same for her about-to-be son and grandson-in-law. "How did I miss your ring when you came in? Wait. Let me see first. Oh, how gorgeous. Oh Mike. Beautiful."

"Hated to take it off, Mom, but Jimmy and Mike and I had to talk first. This decision involves Jimmy more than any of us."

Jimmy shouted, "Mommy!" and ran into Meg's arms with such energy that Meg went into tears of love. So did Mo.

Lots of hugs while Mike asked, "What do a couple of fellas have to do around here to get a little breakfast?" Sort of like John Wayne in *The Quiet Man*.

Mo said, "Shush you, but here's a hug and kiss anyway you brute. Stealing me daughter away from me."

They all laughed, and Jimmy said, "You can talk Irish too, Aunt Mo. Just like Daddy."

It was a great day.

The next day, Sunday, was even better, and Mike and Jimmy picked up Meg for the nine-thirty Mass, and Mo, who wanted to go along with them. They were relieved to not run into any of the Torellis, not knowing the moods they'd be in and not yet wanting to let them know of the engagement. After the service, they stopped at Marie's grave and straightened out the Christmas arrangement they had left, and another left by Fran and Thomas, and went back to Mike and Jimmy's apartment for a big breakfast.

By late morning they began making calls to let relatives, then close friends, know of their big news, and the day became all the more festive. Mike and Jimmy called their relatives, and Meg called hers, and Jimmy got on the phone when Carmen and Regina and others asked for him. Fran and Thomas weren't home, but when they hadn't called back after several hours, it was clear there might, again, be more problems with them.

After Jimmy's nap, they all dropped Mo at her condo on their way to Meg's apartment for dinner, and when they got to Meg's they were astonished to find a huge arrangement of flowers from one of New Haven's most pricey florist shops, sitting on the welcome mat right outside her door.

"Oh, Mike," Meg said. "You must have ordered these last week. How did you know I'd accept your proposal? Pretty sure of yourself I'd say."

"Not from me," Mike said with a big grin. "I don't have that kind of money. Jimmy, help me lift this huge bunch of flowers."

The delivery envelope read, "To Meg Donlon," and on the card inside was written, "All best wishes to both of you. Love, Stan."

"I don't understand," Meg said. "Who told him? How did these get here?"

Mike couldn't believe what he was seeing. "Who the hell does this guy think he is? Who does he think we are? Our big day, and he jumps in. It's outrageous."

"Stan's just a show off, Mike. Besides, flowers go to girls, not guys. I'm the special girl here. I've got the ring, so I get the flowers. You know that. Here, I'll take the flowers in. And please don't get upset about this."

"Yeah, well I am upset, and I also know there's no delivery on Sundays so that means he had to drive all the way down here, pick them up, and then drive over to give them to you himself. That's way out of line. He had to figure you'd be alone. What's that all about? Why couldn't he have just let them be delivered tomorrow? I'm going to straighten him out."

"Not now, Mike. Let's just get dinner started and talk about this later. Jimmy, would you please turn on the TV while I'm in the kitchen? That's a good boy; here, let me take your coat and mittens." Meg scowled at Mike over her shoulder, then turned back to kiss Jimmy's cheek.

"Thanks, Mommy. I can't wait to see your flowers." And he scampered out of the hall into Meg's guest bedroom, which was used as a den for people and a home for the television.

"Mike, you have to calm down about Stan. You make it sound like he's up to something rotten. What makes you get this way? Everyone knows we're head over heels in love, even Stan 'the bachelor.' How about putting some of your excess energy into a big hug and kiss for me, big guy? And just forget about Stan."

Their embrace worked its usual magic on Mike, but Meg knew this was going to be a subject that Mike wouldn't be letting go that easily. "Let me get some dinner started, Mike. Why don't you check in with Jimmy. I'm boiling up some store-bought spaghetti, then making it magnificent with some of Maman Fran's famous tomato sauce. Sound good?"

"Yeah, I guess. Might as well get the Torellis into the mix now that I'm on a roll." Mike shrugged, took a couple of steps towards the TV room, turned back, grinned, and said, "How about one of those Guinness Stouts I left here a couple of months ago?"

"Mike, I tossed them out during that bad time you had, but I do have a bit of Scotch if you promise you'll be good."

"God bless you, darling. Fix me one with water, and come and visit us in the den."

As it turned out, the spaghetti was extraordinary with the Fran Torelli sauce plus odd slices of Rye bread to which Meg gave an Italian flavor by sparking them up with some garlic salt and butter. And since Mike was doing so well, his whisky made their little dinner together a warm, celebratory, and loving high point to a new beginning for the three of them.

"Jimmy," Mike said after dinner, "how about a little nap for you before we go home? Good idea?" Jimmy yawned once, and that was all he needed to totter into Meg's bedroom and sprawl into a sound sleep on her bed.

Mike spread a comforter over Jimmy, kissed the top of his head, and stopped in the kitchen for another Scotch on his way back to Meg who asked, "Are you sure you want that, Mike?"

"Course not. I need it. All I really want is you and Jimmy and Mo and the four of us to be together and happy. And I really need all of that more than anything else. But now I've got this Stan jerk getting in my way and trying to run off with you, Meg, the love of my life. So yeah, I need this Scotch to settle me down...to calm me...to get Stan off my frontal lobe. I'm calling him right now. That little prick."

When Mike had come out of the kitchen, he had snuggled up to Meg on the small sofa in her living room and, as he said this, she dropped her head and began to softly cry. "So what's the deal? You want me to go easy on big shot Stan? What's all the crying for? I'm telling you I'm calling him now. You feel sorry for this dope?"

"Please don't call him, Mike. No one feels sorry for Stan. He sent the flowers to both of us. Who cares if he drove by himself to be the first to congratulate us? Stan is Stan. Maybe he needs to do things like this to feel good about himself. You and I don't have to worry about stuff like that." Then, "Mike. Mike, are you okay? Mike, come back."

Mike had shuffled back to the kitchen and was pouring out the rest of the Scotch into his glass. Meg was horrified to see there had been much more in the bottle than she had realized and that she had actually helped him go over the edge.

"I'm back. Here I am...back. And here's where I'm supposed to be—with you. And with Jimmy. Can't deal with people who fight with me. Need you to help me, Meg."

"You are all I need, Mike. You know I love you. And love Jimmy, too. What are you saying? You trust me, don't you?"

Mike was sinking now but did his best with, "Course I trust you, Meg. Don't trust that prick. Why's he going after you? Why are you letting him? His fancy antique joint. And his big shot flowers... he's trying to make me look like a fool. I'm right, Meg. Why is this? I have to stop him."

With that, Mike slumped over onto Meg's lap, and after a couple unsuccessful minutes trying to revive him, she pulled an Afghan over him and sadly left him to check on Jimmy and softly cry herself to sleep.

Mike was out cold Monday morning as Meg awakened Jimmy, gave him some Raisin Bran and banana slices and combed his hair before taking him over to Mo's for the day. "Why is Daddy still asleep, Mommy? Did he stay up too late?"

"He'll be okay, Jimmy. Just has a little headache from all the excitement yesterday. I'll wake him up for work after I drop you at Aunt Mo's. How do you like the flowers?" Meg had been up early to check on both of her men and took the wrapping off the arrangement, which featured two levels of dozens of bright daffodils and fern fronds mixed in. *Gorgeous*, she thought. *Just what you'd expect from Stan.* She was pleased, despite Mike's outburst, and was praying he would be over that this morning.

When she returned from Mo's, where Jimmy described the lavish display of Stan's flowers and Meg mouthed to her mother, "I'll tell you about it later," Mike was just coming out of the bathroom, hair slicked down from his shower and smoothing down the front of yesterday's dress shirt, now wrinkled as an old dollar bill.

"You're too good for me, Meg Donlon, and I know it, sure." There was no zany grin or boyish attempt to toss off the shame he felt. "I'm sorry. Again. What did Jimmy say?"

"First, Mike, please realize I was as much at fault as you last night. We just can't leave anything around that will derail you. We should know better. You could give me a kiss to start the day though, Mike." And then, "Hey! What kind of a kiss do you call that? That's more like a peck on the cheek I'd say."

Mike had seen Stan's flowers on the living room table and was tightening up. "I don't like those, Meg. Keep them if you want, but I'm not happy with them. And I'm not happy with Stan. You..."

"Oh, for God's sake, I can't believe this. Just go to work. I'll get rid of these right now, and maybe I'll tell you about your son when you get a grip on yourself." Meg snatched the kitchen trash pail, pulled off its swing top, and strode past Mike to the flowers. "The hell with these." She tossed the whole arrangement, vase, flowers, water, and all into the trash. "How's that? Better?"

"Yeah. Yeah it is, Meg. That's better. And that's the first thing you should have done twelve hours ago. That would have been just the thing to do. That prick."

"Mike, I'm done with this. You do what you want. I'm late for work." She kept her grip on the trash pail as her left hand reached for her purse and keys, and she brushed past Mike toward the door. "I'll see you at the station."

"Hey, what's this? You're pissed at me? You're just taking off like I did something wrong? That's bullshit, Meg, and you know it. Go ahead; I don't care where you go. Go see Stan. Go ahead."

With that, Meg burst through the door, slammed it, then burst into tears. She dumped the entire Rubbermaid container down the wall-mounted garbage chute and sped down the stairs and out of the building.

Unbelievably, she could hear Mike yelling the whole way, "Yeah, that's right, you keep those friggin' flowers. Take them with you. Call and tell me how Stan is. No, don't."

CHAPTER TWENTY-THREE

Certain he was in the right, Mike couldn't shed the position he had taken, and his anger continued. He did tidy Meg's apartment a bit—Jimmy's bed and room, the sofa he had slept on, and the bathroom. Then he went out without leaving a note and headed over to Mo's to see Jimmy. Mo was just pulling out of her condo parking space, taking Jimmy to school, as Mike drove in, and she could see he was as angry as Meg had described in her brief phone call. *Oh my,* Mo thought. *It's tough to be head over heels in love.*

Mike pulled into her now empty space, opened her door to give Jimmy a kiss, then hopped into the back seat to ride with them. Leaning into the front, Mike kissed Mo on the cheek saying, "I'm in trouble, Mo."

"Well, Mike, your fiancée happens to think she's in trouble too. But if you want my opinion—and you've never had one from me before—I'd say you've got to let this Stan thing go and chalk it up to a bad dream. Meg says you both agreed on no more bad nights, correct?"

"Did you have a bad dream, Daddy?" Jimmy strained under his seat restraint to peer between the bucket seats.

"I did, Jimmy, like you have sometimes. Like we both had when

Mommy died. Remember? But we said our prayers then, and we felt better, right?" Jimmy solemnly nodded. "So I've said some prayers and now I'm feeling better. What are you doing at school today?"

"We have 'What I Did,' Daddy. After long weekends we get to tell everyone. And I have the best. Guess what?"

"Your sleepover at Aunt Mo's," Mike said.

"Daddy, I do that lots. This time I got a new mommy. That's the best."

Mike's pretend bad dream turned into a reality as Jimmy's pride and excitement and love rushed at him and slapped him as he realized the enormity of his doubly bad behavior. "That is the best, Jimmy. I'm proud of you; aren't you, Aunt Mo?"

"Yes I am, and I'll bet Meg will be thrilled when you call her at work to tell her, Mike. Good for you, Jimmy."

They walked Jimmy to his Kindergarten room where he almost rushed to join his friends but remembered to pause and kiss his father and Aunt Mo goodbye.

On their drive back to pick up Mike's car there were a couple of minutes of silence; then, "I'm going to have to face the music, Mo. Not going to be fun."

"Tell me what it is about Stan, Mike. What's bugging you?"

"Mo, I think he makes me jealous. I know it, and I have been since he made a move on Marie at our engagement party, for God's sake. Did Meg tell you that? Probably not, but I can't forget it. He's rich, eligible, sophisticated, and I don't come close. So I first feel intimidated, and then I worry he's going to get between Meg and me like he tried with Marie."

"Yes, Meg told me about that...a long time ago, and that's a dysfunction with Stan. But I'd say you're the one who's turning this nuisance into a problem. Just look how you let him push the two of you apart this morning. I can understand how you think Stan is nervy, but I really don't see how you can make the leap from a bunch of flowers to an attempt to ruin your relationship."

"Yeah, but..."

"As far as sophisticated and rich, Mike, how can you let things like that bother you? He's also an arrogant snob who probably goes about intimidating all the people he can because it amuses him. You think Meg could ever fall for someone like that? Give her some credit. And don't call her when you get to work; go right into her office, kiss her, and sit down. Then agree to lunch and meet her at noon to re-start your engines. Sound good?"

Mike grinned. "You'll be a great mother-in-law. Probably could have been a great army general for all I know. Thanks. See you tonight."

By one o'clock, at The Beanery, Mike had told Meg about Mo's appraisal of Stan and his own understanding and agreement. Also, he confessed his realization that he was letting himself get too worked up, irrational and, finally, emotionally unbalanced. Finally, that all this had happened because he was a boozer, which they both realized and knew they had to fix.

"What can we do, Mike? I was really scared this morning. About everything. About you and Jimmy. About me. I was frantic about us. I was shaking thinking I might have to leave the station if we broke up. I couldn't stop crying. We can't do that again."

"And we won't. The one way I can get rid of this crazy thing I've got about losing you to Stan is... oh Hell, Meg, let's get married right away. Want to?"

"Do you think so, Mike? Are you sure?"

"Of course, we're in love... wait. You're not sure, Meg?" Mike's initial joy was dashed. "I'm not right for you, Meg? Is it Jimmy? Oh, Meg."

"You and Jimmy are perfect for me, Mike. All I ever hoped for, and I love you both as much as I can."

"What is it then? This morning?" Mike was somber; crushed.

"Mike, I've dreamed about us being married for so long. I was so unhappy years ago. Then I was happy for you and Marie, and I just let go. So I'm knocked over I guess. With love...it must be love. And relief, too. It's just I never thought it would happen so wonderfully like this. Should we be rushing like this? What about...?"

Mike's face lit up with his flashing eyes and boyish, Irish grin, and he put his right arm around Meg's shoulders and pulled her to him, causing other patrons to look up as her chair legs scrapped across the floor.

They kissed, and Meg's own gleaming smile assured Mike she agreed. For both of them it seemed that they had really shed that morning's awful experience and were setting off completely unfettered by all the bogies that had been nipping at them. They were joyous and held hands on their walk back to the station, during which they ducked behind a garage to kiss again, madly and passionately.

In his office, Mike had trouble settling down to work. The pile of avails requests from ad agencies and advertisers was almost a foot high; lots of other paper, memos, faxes; crazy station bulletins; network announcements, and more.

He tried to slow down to exult in their decision to wed at once but was troubled by his mind's inclination to wander back to Stan. Switching between coffee and Pepsi seemed to discourage thoughts about booze, but he was troubled nevertheless.

Meg buzzed him and phoned him every half hour to be sure Mike was sure, which he was, and her excitement was exhilarating for him and just the tonic he needed to reinforce his growing confidence that he could win his battles with insecurity and alcohol.

Mo of course was on cloud nine, which is where all brides' mothers go. Jimmy didn't get what all the excitement was about but did his best to be and act as enthusiastic as the others, and the word about the imminent wedding got out to family, friends, and co-workers in a few days.

Mike's sister and brother-in-law, Mary and Tom, were absolutely thrilled at the news, and Tom was surprised but delighted to be asked to be Best Man. Mo agreed to be Matron of Honor, and she too was delighted. The wedding was to be held on Saturday morning, just four days away, and making arrangements shifted into high gear.

Naturally, Jimmy would present the rings, and he couldn't wait. "This will be perfect for another 'What I Did,'" he confided in his father and about-to-be new mommy.

Mike called Father Bellini, pastor of St. Vincent's, who couldn't be happier; he had three weddings that morning but agreed to perform the nuptials at half past noon. And he promised to request from the Bishop a waiver of the Banns of Marriage ordinarily announced on consecutive weeks at least six months prior to the Sacrament of Marriage. (Mike had hastily volunteered that there was no "physical" necessity for speed, meaning a pregnant bride, and Father Bellini blushed red and said, "Thank you, Michael, the Bishop will be pleased.")

Phone calls went to all the picnic celebrants, plus friends at work, close neighbors, and folks like Christmas Tree Charlie. Mike reserved the party room at Phelan's for the luncheon reception; Mo shopped for a wedding dress with Meg (both agreed on a smart, but reserved, multi-functional suit instead); and Meg went into high gear thinking about honeymoon destinations.

It was also agreed that bridesmaids and ushers were unnecessary; Father Bellini suggested they enjoy the use of the flowers, which would be intentionally left by the couple to be wed at eleven o'clock; Mo offered her own wedding ring, but Meg and Mike had time to shop for their own and found a nice set for both of them Friday morning.

Deciding where the three of them would live post-Honeymoon was over-looked until Mo asked Wednesday night, "So where's your new love nest going to be?"

"Well, we...uh, don't know, I guess," Meg said, turning to look at Mike, and Mike nodded in blank agreement. The silence suggested that they both realized Meg's apartment was too small for the three of them; clearly Mike's place wasn't an option because of the lingering presence Marie's ghost would continue to have.

"I've been thinking about this, and I'll make you two an offer that's so good even I can't refuse." Meg and Mike stared at Mo as she went on to tell them that maintenance charges for her condo had gotten beyond her control in the past two years, and she needed something less expensive. "So I'd like to swap for your place, Meg. What do you think?"

"Well it's wonderful, Mom, but it's crazy. You love this place. You can't just... "

"Course I love it here, honey, and I know you love it. Point is I'm afraid I'm starting to hate it, and I don't want that. Look, let's try it for a month or two; work out your new family budget, figure the extra costs or, I'll bet, the savings, and then decide. The important thing is there'll be no squabbles about where Jimmy's toys will go in your first full month as newlyweds. Now doesn't that make sense for someone who's crazy?"

Mo's offer and advice raised and erased problems they hadn't even considered, and it was so obvious, and so self sacrificing and generous, that the two of them were stunned. Mike said, "It's like the expression, 'Dying and going to heaven,' Mo. This is beyond anything we could have come up with. Are you really sure?"

She was sure, and they were overwhelmed; Jimmy took it with his innocent aplomb, as if to say, "What did you expect?" So it was decided that right after the wedding Mo's most necessary furnishings would be traded for most of Meg's furniture, accessories, closet contents, and "must haves;" Mo's guest room contents would be left as is so that Jimmy would have use of his usual bed while his dad and new mom were away, and Mike's apartment would be sorted out after they returned from the honeymoon. "You men live out of gym bags anyway," Meg said.

Mary and Tom offered to host a rehearsal dinner at the posh New Haven Club (where they were members) attended by Father Bellini ("I wouldn't miss it," he said), Tom's folks, his and Mary's daughters, Barbara and Martha, his brother, Stan, Mike's folks, and Carmen and Regina. It was explained in a tearful call from Fran Torelli to Mary that she was suffering from migraine headaches, and they were sorry but hoped to be at the wedding.

Everyone was embarrassed for them at this transparent rudeness, particularly when Carmen said she had never in her life seen her mother with a migraine. In the same conversation, Carmen also revealed that she and Regina had stopped accepting baby-sitting assignments, because they were just so ashamed about their mother's behavior and didn't know how to explain it. "Are we forgiven?" asked Carmen.

"Nothing to forgive," Meg said. "We love you both."

Mike had called Fran and Thomas to ensure that everything was really all right and his former father-in-law answered the phone and reluctantly, it seemed, confirmed the migraines. He sounded worn out though, and beaten down, but was able to ask about Jimmy and happy to learn his grandson was healthy and happy. He offered Mike his very best wishes, and Mike could tell there wasn't a chance Thomas and Fran would show up. *What a shame,* he thought. *Dear, kind Marie would never approve of this.*

Meg, Mike, and Mo all took Friday off—manicures, pedicures, and hair styling for the ladies; haircuts for Jimmy and Mike and collecting freshly cleaned and pressed garments, for the wedding and the honeymoon, at the cleaners who also had altered a little boy's suit for Jimmy.

At a break for tea, Friday afternoon at Mo's, Meg told Mike that she had written a thank you note, from both of them, to Stan for the flowers he had sent. "I'm telling you this now, Mike, so there's no surprise about anything. You know it was the correct thing to do. Besides, we've agreed that episode and Stan are all behind us, and I know it won't come up again. We promised each other."

"I'm glad you did that, Meg. Stan will be happy. And I'll mention them to him myself." Mike smiled broadly and looked from Mo to Meg and back to make sure he had handled that properly, and neither tried to hide their deep exhalation of relief. This let them all laugh, take another deep breath together and, with renewed resolve, put the matter to rest.

* * * * *

Father Bellini had everyone in big grins during the rehearsal at St. Vincent's with his recollections about things that had gone wrong during weddings... funny stories about grooms showing up at the wrong church, the rings getting lost, an elderly guest fainting during the ceremony and falling flat in the aisle 15 feet from the altar, choir boys singing the wrong song. A very funny man, a good, holy priest, and utterly reassuring that their wedding would be perfect.

The Friday dinner at the club was lavish and lovely with lots of family anecdotes about Meg as a younger girl, and boyfriends who didn't work out, Mike's high notes and low notes, some rakish toasts, and a lovely tribute from Mo to her daughter, which brought the tears and hankies out.

The wedding was perfect, as Father Bellini said it would be, and Jimmy was the picture of control and proud as he could be with his part in it all. Carmen had quietly told Mike and Meg before the proceedings began that her parents weren't coming and that took care of a small anxiety they had not been able to shake. And to top it all, even though there had been no invitations sent out, about 75 friends, co-workers, old buddies, whatever, showed up and took up pews in the back half of the church. And they led a round of applause as the ceremony ended; Meg and Mike kissed, stepped off the altar, and recessed from the church with smiles and best wishes from everyone.

It was becoming the best of the "great days" they seemed to have been blessed with, with fun and back slaps, and lots of praise for Jimmy, and all the hugs and kisses that the Irish Catholics can't seem to get through a day without. These are hugs and kisses that their Protestant brethren find agreeably quaint to participate in on special occasions. When they do so, it is with a fervor that suggests they could convert for at least a day, if the subject came up.

Waving thanks and goodbyes to all their "back-of-the-church" friends, their one limousine and eight other cars made the trip into New Haven and Phelan's Pub in less than ten minutes.

"Daddy, what's wrong?" said Jimmy, as their small, white limo pulled up in front of Phelan's. At that, the laughing and joking Mo, Meg, and Mike looked out the tinted limo window to see Phelan's sidewalk lined with even more people clapping, cheering, toasting and, suitably, hugging and kissing.

Most in the crowd they knew or at least recognized; others were complete strangers, but all seemed to be really celebrating their arrival. And then they saw the banner across the front: "Phelan's Loves Jimmy, Meg, Mike, and Mo. Cead Mille Failte."

The sentiment was generous and, typically, their eyes began to water, except Jimmy's who asked, "Why are you so sad? Your friends make me feel happy."

"We're happy too, Jimmy. All these friends are saying they are happy for all of us. It's a surprise and that makes tears of joy. And see the Irish words on the sign? They say 'A Hundred Thousand Welcomes.' That's the best thing to hear when you're Irish. Or anyone. Come on, let's go shake some hands."

So for the next quarter hour, the bridal party of four worked back and forth through all those wonderful greeters shaking hands. Handshakes, backslaps, random kisses, and hugs with unknowns, flash cameras in their faces...it was like any St. Patrick's Day Parade except with Mo as the Grand Marshall and Jimmy the Leprechaun.

As all this was going on, the Dickinsons, Flynns, Torelli girls, Father Bellini...all the invited guests, found an open and easy path into Phelan's where beer, wine or whiskey were thrust immediately into their hands. No Champagne today; this was far too important an occasion—this celebrated the salt of the earth!

Meg was aglow with excitement, pleasure, and love—for Mike and Jimmy, of course, but in such a big way for all these wonderful friends of Mike's (mostly) and hers, and Mike's and hers (from the station), who joined with them.

Phelan's had room for just about a third of them, but that didn't seem to matter. When the wedding party finally went inside, the outside celebrants cheered and applauded some more and went off to more parties of their own at another place.

The reception was overwhelming with more love, laughter, and dance than any of them could recall having ever enjoyed before. Mo, Meg, and Jimmy were as sparkly as imaginable. And Mike was dry as toast and loving every minute.

Luncheon was really a full-blown dinner—what the Irish call "Tea"—and featured corned beef, cabbage, carrots, boiled potatoes, Irish soda bread, lots of Guinness. But no tea except for Mike, Meg, and Jimmy. The toasts were outrageous, close to blasphemous, hard on Jimmy's ears, but hysterically funny.

Setting the tone was the good Father, himself, who led his own toast with, "As an Italian I knew I was in the wrong place when I got here and the Gaelic banner out front said, 'It's All Your Fault.' That's what it says, doesn't it?" Lots of boos and laughter followed this.

"Well be assured, it's not my fault; I've been absolutely celibate for thirty-seven years. Mike Flynn is somebody else's fault!" The place went crazy.

Finally Father Bellini said, "I had a Bishop once who told me, 'Always leave them laughing'—so I'm out of here." Then he turned to face the bride and family, blessed them, and made a quarter turn to bless all of the guests. Quite a lovely, ecumenical gesture and, who knows, maybe pressed the right buttons for some.

With the tone set, other toasts and mini-speeches prevailed (good thing Jimmy fell fast asleep) and, as another attack of hunger reared up at five-thirty, Phelan's emptied quickly and the close-in relatives chatted happily together.

"So where's the happy couple honeymooning?" asked Stan. A chorus of voices said, "That's right! Who knows? Where are you going? How long?" Even Mike didn't know the plans Meg had made.

"It's a secret," Meg said. "But if we don't leave in the next ten minutes, change into warmer-weather sports clothes, and get to the airport in the next forty-five minutes, there will be a double available tonight, probably at a highly reduced rate, in Bermuda."

Mike's yelp when he heard that awakened Jimmy, who sat up as his father was kissing his new mother, and the family group was clapping. With Mo, the four of them whisked out and to Mo's (now former) apartment where they quickly changed and then drove less than fifteen minutes to the Tweed Airport, inside the East Haven town line, about ten blocks from St. Vincent's.

Their non-stop, six-thirty plane, direct to the Hamilton Airport in Bermuda, was scheduled to put them on the ground at eight-fifty.

CHAPTER TWENTY-FOUR

Despite the short trip, their flight attendant easily detected they were celebrating more than an anniversary, confirmed that in a quick, whispered conversation with Meg, and then presented them with two Champagne splits. "Courtesy of the Captain," she said. And a few minutes later the captain himself strode straight to them from the cockpit, beaming with good wishes, shaking hands with other passengers along the way, then stopped and boomed, "Well, it's Mr. and Mrs. Michael Flynn, if I live and breathe. Last time I saw you, Michael, your parents thought you'd never get out of the ninth grade. And now look at you—married to the prettiest girl I've ever seen." The plane erupted in laughter first, then cheers, and then applause when the pilot leaned over to kiss Meg on the cheek.

Suddenly they heard Mike say, "Thanks, Captain, but I don't remember you. Where did you live?"

The captain said, "In a small town outside Chicago, but this is the only way I get to kiss the new brides." The passengers were beside themselves with their laughter and this joke on Mike and began to shout, "More! More! More! More!"

Mike and Meg stood, waved to all, bowed, shook the captain's hand, (he kissed Meg a second time) and settled down, feeling very special and happy to be with each other. Forever.

* * * * *

January temperatures in Bermuda are crisp after dark—more than cool—but the enclosed van sent by the Southampton Princess Hotel, barely a half hour from the airport was comfortable, and their cheerful driver made the trip seem just a few minutes.

The Princess stands ten stories above a knoll already one hundred and ten feet above sea level, and the night sky was bright with the Milky Way. Bermuda's two "cities," Hamilton and St. George, never put out much light—the Bermuda charm is low key—so even if guests were in rooms that faced the west, they would see just dots of lights like a decorously trimmed Christmas tree.

As it was, the eastern shoreline was less than fifty yards from the Princess' pool, and then it was all Atlantic Ocean to Ireland—and dead black, save for the stars.

The trip from New Haven plus van ride plus check-in took just over three hours, and the two of them weren't at all tired. More like the exhilaration that comes from an adrenaline high.

Meg's "Honeymoon Suite" arrangements comprised a corner room with an L-shaped balcony to the east and south, king-size bed, in-room Jacuzzi-equipped tub, a fruit basket, cheese, crackers, and a nice Chardonnay. The ambiance was soft, quiet (January is a very quiet month in Bermuda), and lovely as they sat outside recalling their day. No dining room or room service; the basket treats would be plenty.

Meg was warmed to her core seeing that Mike wasn't interested at all—it seemed—in the wine. Two sips from the glass Meg had poured, and he set it aside. "You're a rascal, Mrs. Flynn. How did you pull all this off without going crazy wanting me to know your secret? You are my amazing wife."

After an extended embrace with Mike getting a bit fresh and Meg daring him to, "try that again and see what happens," which he did, and more of the same happening, Meg came up for air.

"My mom is great at secrets, honey. And she asked me only about details like how far away, hot, cold or medium, city, country or seashore—you know, the big stuff. My contributions were things like king not queen, for sleeping; Jacuzzi would be nice; departure city New Haven, not New York. Do you like it?"

"The best—like you!"

"She didn't tell me that this is what she had arranged until two days ago. And that was to make sure I could pack stuff she overlooked. She even had some of my spring things dry-cleaned, and she got clothes out of your closet, which she put in my bag."

"Like what?"

"Your favorite pajamas, for example. Tops, no bottoms."

Well, that did it. Mike said, "You know, I've been wearing extra-long tees for the past five years. I don't think those pajamas even fit me anymore."

"Oh, too bad," Meg said. "Want to try them?"

After a sudsy splash in the Jacuzzi, Meg was happy to learn Mike was correct about his pajamas. "Good thing too," was the last thing Meg heard as they both drifted off.

* * * * *

Bermuda is a lovely, quiet, soothing, genteel place to be in any season. The heritage of many of the island's residents goes back hundreds of years; tourists who fly in are often regulars and thoroughly respectful of local customs; the giant cruise ships discharge passengers who instantly seem to grasp the island's sweet, civilized behavior and adapt at once. So in January, with far fewer people, one experiences even more of the same.

For these honeymooners it was a first visit, but they were agreeably in Bermuda-tune at once. And they felt no urge to visit the touristy, but still reserved, Perfume Factory or the Coral Cavern or Fort Adams. Neither played golf but nevertheless hugely enjoyed their early morning traipses over the still green and springy nine-hole golf course, which filled the peninsula upon which the Princess was perched. The never-ending ocean enchanted them and provoked the not-unusual wonder for most tourists: *Why do we want to go home?*

In addition to the golfing and the pink coral sand beaches, visitors to Bermuda spend a lot of time on tennis courts, which seem to be everywhere, and touring the island on bicycles, motorbikes, and modified golf carts. The advantages? All are easy to drive on the left side of the streets—they're wide open to the sun and sea breezes and can be parked nearly everywhere on the island.

So—for any of the sports, shops, restaurants, experimenting with new beaches, the open-air vehicles are chosen most often, and most young people from eighteen up to their late forties go for the motorbikes first. And that's what the Flynns did.

Everywhere you go, everyone you pass—residents and visitors alike—smile, say hello, or wave. All this includes the smartly uniformed policemen and women who help vehicles get through the roundabouts without accident. These cheery traffic directors dress in dark blue skirts or shorts atop the ubiquitous knee-high Bermuda socks, starched short sleeved shirts, a blue tie, and a snappy white police cap with a broad blue band and shiny black brim. All so civilized!

Meg usually started off letting Mike lead the way, and when in light traffic she'd speed past him with a laugh. She relished their togetherness and let her thoughts wander over how fortunate she was to have Mike and Jimmy. And how perfect their love truly was.

Mike readily assumed the personality and charm of a perfect tourist and was happy and patient whether in a checkout line or waiting for a restaurant table to clear; and complimenting Meg on the numerous shorts and sweaters she'd try on in deciding her preference. Meg committed herself to always remember how good Mike really was inside, down deep, even when he might take a step backwards and totter a bit.

Their stay was to end on Friday, a full five nights so they could be home in time to reorganize over the weekend and get back to work Monday morning as promised. One call home daily was their agreement, about dinner time, and Jimmy and Mo looked forward to that and were prepared with lots of news.

Mostly though, Jimmy had his own adventures to report, and the honeymooners were relieved their separation created no disturbance. Mo agreed that he was perfectly at ease and well behaved—as usual. What she wanted to know about was Bermuda. "Is the Princess perfect? What about the food? Are the people nice? Do you have the right clothing?"

"Well fortunately," Meg said, "Mike's pajamas don't fit him very well anymore." Mo howled with laughter, which Mike could hear across the room.

As their Thursday night came to a close, Mike said, "Jimmy sounded a little down, Mo. Anything go wrong today?"

"Not really. He seemed a little tired when I picked him up this afternoon. I took his temperature when we got home and that was up a bit. About 100°, but 99.2° is usual for a five year old, so..."

"Did you call the doctor?"

"Oh no, Mike. This is probably just a little bug. His teacher said two other children had elevated temps last week and are fine."

"Yeah, but Jimmy has never been sick, Mo; must have Marie's Italian resistance. So it's hard for me to say, 'Oh, okay.' Are you sure?"

"He's not cranky, Mike. The same wonderful Jimmy you left with me; just a little tired. But look, I'll keep him out of school anyway, and we'll see the doctor. That way you and Meg will have nothing to worry about when you arrive. Still about five at the airport, right?"

"Great, Mo. Love you. Here's Meg...and don't ask about the pajamas."

CHAPTER TWENTY-FIVE

At dinner Meg assured Mike that her mother was completely at ease about Jimmy. "You know, Mike, the old twenty-four-hour bug. But Mom wants you to share her confidence. So let's move on."

"Right," agreed Mike. And they spent that night reliving every happy moment since they'd met...lots of fast forwards...and they thoroughly reviewed the wedding, the party, their honeymoon trip—all of it.

At one point Mike pointed out that "sweetie" had become a new pet name since Meg had agreed that his pajamas no longer fit. It was "sweetie-pie" from Meg when he pretended, for example, to be sinking in the Jacuzzi. Sort of like, "Oh, poor sweetie-pie, let me help you up. Oh, what have we here? I see that you already are. For Heaven's sake..." And that sort of thing went on until, let's say, sleep took them over.

Looking back the next morning, the thing that most pleased and impressed them and held out the most hope for the future was their combined beverage consumption. Sips of Chardonnay on arrival were their first and last indulgence with beverage alcohol. Water, juice, tea, coffee, and more (English) tea had taken charge and become their preferences as well.

They spent the early part of their last day as usual: the early stroll over the heavily be-dewed golf course; a short, delicious, and animated breakfast in the Princess' lower Terrace Room, then the fast and fun open-air bus ride into Hamilton for all the souvenirs they would need and cute, handy, maybe goofy, gifts for their friends at home.

For Jimmy they bought a beautiful Conch shell. Since US import laws prohibited this if the core had not been drilled by the Conch's enemy, the ocean squid, they were careful to assure theirs was legal. More importantly though, they had huge new subject matter for Jimmy to explain and demonstrate to his classmates.

Much of what they bought was non-essential, but chic; bargain-priced sweaters and shorts, and tees were always fun. For Mo they purchased a lovely, tightly woven "Bermuda Bag," a purse with Cedar handles, well-known worldwide as the official icon of this mid-Atlantic island of charm.

The Princess graciously offered "late departure," assuming the couple would want to check out no earlier than "half after two" for their return flight to Tweed, and the Flynns were delighted. After their morning shopping, noon buffet lunch, and time to pack, use up the rest of the gratuitous "body lotions," briefly "nap," dress, and catch the airport vans, they were more than delighted with The Princess' offer; perhaps astonished.

At check-in they were further astonished that their airline, British Air, had upgraded them to first class. "Probably the same captain we had on the flight over," Mike said. And it was. He welcomed them aboard and hoped they would return another time.

Once airborne, they wondered about Jimmy's visit to the doctor and how he was doing. No word from Mo was a relief. Or was it? They agreed it was.

When no one met them at Tweed, Meg's call to her mom revealed that she was concerned about Jimmy and uneasy about bringing him with her to the airport or leaving a sitter with him.

"Damn, Mom. What's wrong?"

"Nothing's wrong, honey. He's fine. Just get your bags and a taxi and we'll welcome you with open arms in less than thirty minutes. Love you." And Mo rang off.

When Meg and Mike's elevator got up to the floor of Mo's former apartment, they were delighted with the bunch of balloons floating in the lobby area and a large poster (design by Mo, color by Jimmy) taped over the lobby mirror. Not the usual "Welcome Home" though, but "We Missed You!" was the message, and looking down the hall they saw Jimmy and Mo standing outside the open door of their new apartment waving, blowing kisses, and shouting cries of welcome.

Their joint relief at seeing a spirited and obviously happy Jimmy in pajamas, bathrobe, and slippers, with Mo's hand on his shoulder and a huge grin on her face, let them drop their bags, totes, and all, and rush the forty feet down the hall to hug and kiss with their usual "all-together-now" zeal.

"Mommy, Mommy, I love you! Daddy, what did you bring me? And Mo?"

Lots of hugs and kisses, Jimmy. We saved them up." And Meg used her hug to lift him so that she and Mike could both squeeze him between them. Mike gently began his tickle routine, and Jimmy squealed with fun. Love was everywhere, but Meg could see some unusual lines in Mo's forehead.

"Let's go in, Mike; maybe Jimmy will help you with the bags. Be careful of the big one with Jimmy's present in it." Meg said this with a smile as a tease for Jimmy.

"Come on, Daddy." Jimmy raced back to the bags, grabbed the biggest one, and tried to drag it down the hall. "I'll take that one, Jimmy. This one is a gift for Aunt Mo. Do you want to give it to her?"

"Yes, Daddy!" Jimmy was at once relieved to leave the heavy bag behind and pleased to bear Mo's gift into the living room. He quickly took the smaller tote from his dad and, when he turned away, Mike saw an unusual red swelling behind and beneath Jimmy's right ear.

"Wait, Jimmy. That will wait. How about another squeeze for me?"

Jimmy sighed in exasperation but went back to his father who said, "What's this bump, Jimmy? Did you fall at school? Does it hurt?"

"That's nothing, Daddy. The doctor said I'm fine, but I think we have to see him again."

Then Jimmy raced off with Mo's gift tote, and Mike felt a spike in his pulse rate. He pushed it down and joined the others to find snacks and sodas, brownies and milk, and tea or coffee. It all seemed perfect. And when he asked Mo about Jimmy's bump she simply said, "Not sure, Mike, but it's not sore so we have to watch it, that's all."

Meg handed Jimmy his gift first but, typically, he said, "Oh no. Aunt Mo has to open hers first. She deserves it." And he put his aside for a moment.

Mo loved her Bermuda Bag. "This will knock them over at Channel 5. I can't wait for warmer weather to show this off."

With slow and formal ceremony Jimmy accepted his larger, square carton, slowly untied and unwrapped it, and screeched with delight when the one-pound Conch shell tumbled out onto the carpeting. "Look, Aunt Mo, a Genie shell. I can get three wishes from the Genie in here."

"Genies live in brass lamps, Jimmy. Find an old brass lamp, and you might be able to meet a real Genie," Meg said. "But I read somewhere that all the real Genies have been found and have disappeared. This is a Conch shell, and when you hold it up to your ear you can hear the ocean. Try it."

Everyone went silent as Jimmy did what Meg suggested, and his eyes widened in delight as he heard the sound. "Aunt Mo, Mommy; listen. We're on the beach. You can hear the waves. Daddy, put your ear in here!"

So they all repeated the seashell ritual that had been shown to them by Jimmy's initiation to the "magic of the shell" and were magically and wonderfully taken back to his age, or a year or two older or younger, when they were first enchanted by the same mystery.

"Mommy, Daddy, will this work at school, or do I have to have all the other kids out here by the ocean to listen?" Reassurances followed but stopped short of letting Jimmy also know that holding one's ear to an ordinary coffee cup would produce nearly the same phenomenon.

After enjoying Mo's always-traditional lasagna for birthdays, holidays, homecomings, whatever, Aunt Mo left for Meg's former apartment with Meg walking her down the hallway to the elevator lobby.

"Mike thinks that bump behind Jimmy's ear looks like trouble, Mom. What is that? And why didn't you tell us more about it?"

"I've been waiting until now, honey. This is the kind of news that would put Mike back into a bottle of Scotch, which is not what we need. And your new place doesn't have even an old beer hanging around. So don't let him out to 'buy a newspaper,' okay?"

"What is it, Mom?"

"Doctor Greenway says the bump could be the result of a bump from Jimmy bouncing off something at school or a spider bite or lots of things. With the little jump in his temperature though, it could be more serious. He wants to have Jimmy come to his office tomorrow or Tuesday for a little tissue sample. You know, a biopsy, to see what's going on. But he's not worried at all, and Jimmy seems fine."

"Mom! Why didn't you tell us this? At least me. Suppose it's a tumor? How could you?"

"Meg, honey, I'm telling you. Doctor Greenway thinks it's nothing, and neither do I. Jimmy seems fine. So we wait a couple days and see what the lab says. The real challenge is not upsetting Mike and tipping him over the edge. That's what we have to be careful about. Don't you think Jimmy seems healthy?"

"Oh, Mom, of course. He's the same old Jimmy and seems perfect. What worried Mike after our last call from Bermuda was that Jimmy has never, ever had a temperature, sore throat, 'red eye,' any school-kid illnesses, and he got worried. The lump makes it all the more scary."

"Honey, Doctor Greenway's phone number is on the pad by the fridge. Call the service, and make an emergency appointment, and go in tomorrow or Monday and see."

CHAPTER TWENTY-SIX

When Meg returned to the apartment, Jimmy was sitting in his dad's lap enjoying the twenty photos they'd been able to have developed, plus another couple dozen postcards of shots they would never have been able to take.

"This sand doesn't look white, Daddy. Is it really sand?"

"That's the famous pink sand of Bermuda, Jimmy, and it really doesn't look this pink. But it is rosy. It comes from coral in the ocean."

"What's coral?"

So Mike explained that and more—where conch shells come from, all about the horse-drawn taxis, the white gloves and Bermuda shorts worn by the smiling police, the palm trees, and all the views of the sunrises and sunsets they had taken.

"Are you feeling okay, Jimmy?" Meg put her hand on his forehead, which seemed warm to her. "I think its bedtime, don't you?"

He did and knelt for his prayers and was happy to be tucked in by his dad while Meg began sorting through their bags to get their vacation laundry started.

The washer/dryer combination was conveniently hidden in an

oversized pantry in the kitchen, and Meg could hear the familiar, and now ominous, rattle of ice cubes in a cocktail glass. "Oh, Mike," she said. "Do you really want to?"

"Don't worry, sweetie. Just some tap water. The cubes are to calm me down. What's the story?"

"Mo said Doctor Greenway wants to see Jimmy tomorrow or Monday, and we're to call the service now to confirm a time."

"What are you talking about? The bump on his head or his temperature?"

"Jimmy was a little warm before; I think because of his excitement over us being home. The doctor wants to take a tissue sample from the bump."

"Wait a minute, Meg. This is disturbing me a little; we should have come home."

"I think Monday will be just fine, Mike. Let's not get ourselves worked up. You'll want to get back to the station early. I'll try for an appointment at ten o'clock if you want to come from work to be with us."

They went back and forth recalling "worst cases," with Meg continuously playing down the very worst. She realized Mike could be staggered easily because of Marie's outcome. But Mike seemed to pull himself together, and Meg was relieved.

"No. You're right. I'm not going to get rattled over this. I'm guessing you'll be able to take Jimmy from the doctor's office right back to school—with his Conch shell for "What I Did"—and fill me in when you come in. Phew. I'm sure happy you are the calm parent. And my sweetheart forever!"

But Mike was rattled and was thrown back to the highs, lows, euphoria, and panic as both families hoped, prayed, and rallied each other as Marie slipped, recovered, then slipped some more. A terrible time, and a terrible ending. He knew he was facing two dragons: one, Jimmy's doctors and their diagnoses and two, perhaps more fearful, his own frailty and dependence on alcohol for false strength. This first chased him down during those dark days when Marie at last failed and he sensed he might be in just as much trouble now.

A mild panic began to prod at him. "What do you think, Meg? Could it be just a bump or a bite? What else could it be?"

"We'll know soon, Mike." And when Meg called to make the appointment, the answering service was expecting her call, and the operator was happy to juggle others to fit her and Jimmy in at ten o'clock Monday morning.

"So, that's all set, sweetie. Let's shake off the last of our pink sand and get some sleep. I'll tuck Jimmy in."

Saturday and Sunday offered highs and lows; happy to be home; Meg's job at being Jimmy's "official" mommy by marriage; Jimmy's contentment; Mo's satisfaction in performing well; Meg and Mike's sheer joy as husband and wife; the anxiety of the two-day wait; fears as Jimmy's temperature would shoot up after a slow drop; the nasty look of the bump.

Mo had separated their mail into piles including Bills and Business, News, Notes, Junk, Wedding Wishes, and Welcome Back (from Jimmy). This was fun for the three of them, plus Mo, and the weekend sped by. On Sunday morning they joined together for the nine o'clock Mass at St. Vincent where they were relieved to not see Fran and Thomas so soon after their honeymoon.

On Monday Mike was off to work before dawn, and Meg luxuriated in rolling over for another two hours of sleep before Jimmy awakened.

At the station, Mike was surprised by the "Welcome Back, Meg and Mike" banner and signs and balloons—and delighted. He realized right away that Mo had called one of her old pals and, before leaving, encouraged the entire display, and why not? She had been a twenty-seven-year veteran; Meg had been there almost eleven years and Mike thirteen. *So I guess our nearly fifty years of service earns us three dozen balloons*, he thought.

Dave Batchelder had left notes on his desk suggesting a sales department meeting at eleven o'clock to get Mike up to speed—thoughtful, because it gave Mike several hours to clear off the piles of mail, memos, and general clutter from his desk. And he was able to call most of his clients, many of whom were at least casual friends of his; a few were longtime and solid friends.

The tension that had been growing in him during the short drive to the station eased quickly away, and he thought, *Well, that's what honeymoons and vacations are supposed to do.* He also made a promise to take getaway trips more often. *Why not? No one seems to have had any problems without me.*

He couldn't completely shake off the anxiety associated with Jimmy's ten o'clock appointment, though, or settle the butterflies flitting about in his stomach.

Mo had agreed to help out in Meg's absence today, and when Mike saw her car pull into the parking area just past eight-thirty, he went to the main lobby to meet her. "I would have ordered a much larger banner, Mo, and hundreds of balloons, if it were you getting back from Bermuda. But this is okay." His eyes twinkled, and Mo planted a big kiss on his cheek.

Mike took two cups of coffee out to the reception desk at which Mo had agreed to stand in so that the full-time receptionist, Jenny, could help out in the Traffic Department while Meg took Jimmy to the doctor. He was relieved she already knew from Meg about Jimmy's appointment, and he thanked her for her soothing influence the night before. "Best part getting home, Mo, is your great place. We slept like babies, and it's much better in a bed than on a couch." He added the last line with a wink.

"From what your bride told me this morning, living room couches are off your list of preferred napping areas. Nice going!"

"Thanks, Mo. I really don't know what it was. Neither of us was interested; tea or Pepsi or OJ just seemed, well, better."

"And with our solid sleep last night, today I'm all the more grateful your best judgment told you to let us get home before learning about Jimmy. Thanks. Oh, when did you speak with Meg?"

"Oh God, she went back to sleep after you left and just phoned ten minutes ago. She should be calling back in, let's see, ninety minutes. Go to work!"

* * * * *

Mike began checking the time at ten o'clock and, by Dave's eleven o'clock meeting and no word from Meg, he was losing his forced nonchalance and starting to sweat. "Mo," Mike spoke into his intercom, "you're not holding my calls are you? Any word yet?"

"Nope. I'll interrupt your meeting when she calls, Mike. Not to worry."

But Mike did worry, and ten minutes into the sales meeting the traffic manager, Michelle, had to repeat her question to Mike not once but twice.

"I'm sorry Michelle, I'll call Charlie Martin. I can't believe they don't have their new commercial material here. Did they promise film or tape?"

Michelle was startled. "Mike, they've never sent film; all their stuff is on tape. You remember, right?"

"Yeah, of course. Guess a week away on pink sand in the Atlantic is too much of a good..."

The intercom had buzzed, and Mo was asking Mike to come to reception to take a call. Mike bolted from the room asking Michelle over his shoulder to, "please make the call for me, and remind Charlie his schedule goes on the air Wednesday morning and that Mike needs to know what's up."

When he got to the lobby, Mike thought Mo's bright smile was just a little too flashy to be as carefree as she wanted it to be, so he knew the call was from Meg and asked Mo, "Okay?"

Mo said, "They're still with the doctor, Mike. Use the phone over by the coffee table."

Doing his best, Mike said, "Hey, sweetie, how'd it go? Jimmy okay?"

"Oh sure, honey. But his bump may be a little more serious."

"Serious? What makes the bump serious?"

"Well Doctor Greenway thought he would be dealing with a boil, maybe in the worst case a cyst, so he lanced the bump, and nothing happened."

"What's that mean, Meg? What's supposed to have happened?"

"I don't know, Mike, but something. So then he asked me to wait outside his examining room so he and his assistant could take a tissue sample for a biopsy. He thought I might faint or something."

"Oh jeez. Well what happened? Is Jimmy okay?"

"The doctor said Jimmy's got a tissue mass but not a cyst. So it's a tumor of some sort."

"A tumor? For Christ's sake. So what do we do?"

"It's probably benign, Mike. That's what Doctor Greenway said."

"Probably?"

"The thing is, the lab has to evaluate the tissue, and that takes a couple of days, so Doctor Greenway says the best thing is to operate to take whatever it is out. Then see what the lab finds." And Meg couldn't stand it without Mike there and burst into sobs. "I don't know. Please come and get us, Mike." And she hung up.

Mike could see that Mo understood Meg had news that was more bad than good, and she just nodded and said, "You go, Mike, but take it easy and drive slowly. Want me to drive you?"

"No. I'll be fine. Have to toughen up now for Jimmy and Meg. I'll be fine. We'll call you in a little while. Let Dave and Michelle know." And then, "There'll be an operation of some kind, Mo; I'm thinking it must be in the morning. We'll call. Love you." He kissed her on the forehead and calmly, deliberately (as she had counseled), went back to his office for his briefcase and keys, and then drove to New Haven's Temple Street area where the hundreds of physicians affiliated with Yale-New Haven Hospital maintained their offices.

Parking was easy in the five-story garage on Temple with mid-air walkways to the north, right into the Temple Medical Center. It took a few minutes, but when he found the doctor's office, Meg and Jimmy were relaxing with magazines in the waiting room as though nothing had happened.

Jimmy ran to his dad as soon as the door opened saying, "Look at my bandage, Daddy. It only hurt a little bit. The doctor said I was brave!"

"You are brave, Jimmy. You are the bravest; let me see. Oh, good for you. Here's a kiss. How about a hug? And how about a hug and kiss for

Mommy?" Mike scooped Jimmy up, and the three of them embraced together—Mike easily feeling the tightness in Meg's arms and back and then the slow relaxation as they huddled together. This intimate reunion was so powerful that Meg's initial quavering just stopped—even before Mike was aware that she was close to emotional exhaustion.

Doctor Greenway joined them almost at once, shook hands with Mike, and led them into a small conference room where quartered sandwiches, chips, diet-sodas, and water had been set out.

"Your mom tells me you like ham salad sandwiches best, Jimmy. They're right here on the whole wheat bread. Milk, too?"

"Yes, please. And thank you." Jimmy started right in on his sandwich as the doctor, impressed with the elegance of his young patient's manners, raised his eyebrows in surprise and winked his approval to Meg and Mike.

Mike was getting a good feeling about Doctor Greenway and, under the table, reached for Meg's hand and gently squeezed. He could feel her softening even more and relaxed with her, heartbeat by heartbeat. The three adults all smiled warmly as Jimmy slowly savored two Toll House cookies with his milk.

Over the next twenty minutes Meg and Mike became more and more impressed by, confident in, and fond of Doctor Greenway, now agreed to as Doctor G. for Jimmy and Bill Greenway for them.

The process for treating Jimmy made great sense and involved an "easy surgery" in the morning with Meg and Jimmy spending the night right in the pediatric ward of Yale-New Haven. The procedure couldn't be scheduled before eleven o'clock, but Jimmy's nourishment and water intake would be carefully managed and that was important if any sedation was required.

"We find it important, Mike, to fully sedate our young patients like Jimmy. Sometimes they get an itch or want to look around...you understand." They did. "And Jimmy's 'bump' is really only the size of a pea, so there will be virtually no scarring and almost no post-op discomfort. You realize it's best to just get rid of whatever this is no matter what the lab eventually tells us. Right?"

How could they say no? They were completely comfortable with this remarkably assuring physician and his aura of absolute concern for Jimmy, them— probably all his patients.

It was just two-thirty when Meg promised she would call home before Jimmy went to sleep; then Mike left his wife and son at the hospital to return for a couple of hours to his office. And, of course, to let Mo learn in person that all seemed well under control, positive, and they were all certain they'd be beyond this in a week or two.

Once again Mo had already heard from Meg the schedule for the next day and was, therefore, buoyant and delighted to be able to hug Mike with real joy when he got back to the station.

They agreed that Mike would catch up at his desk, and Mo would visit at Yale-New Haven. Then both would meet at "The Flynn's Place," as they had agreed to call Mo's former apartment, in time for a sandwich supper, which Mo would bring with her, and to speak with Jimmy on the phone as Mike had promised.

* * * * *

"I'll be having just the one, Tim," a beaming Mike announced to his friend Tim Halloran when he strode into Phelan's at five-thirty. Tim's eyebrows had shot up in surprise but professionally flattened as Mike assumed his "usual" bar stool.

"So Mike," Tim asked, "back from your honeymoon then, and Jimmy and the new bride doing well, is it? Everything fine with the family?"

"Will be, Tim. Will be. Thanks for asking, Tim. Small operation for Jimmy tomorrow, and back to normal. Easy as pie. And well it should be with my darling Marie looking down on me and Jimmy. And Meg, of course."

"Sorry to know that. Nothing serious, then?"

"Less than an hour and home the same day."

"Bring them both in the next time. Was it coffee you wanted, Mike.

Or something else?" Tim had been serving Meg and Mike soft drinks and coffee on their last several visits, and his question was direct but non-committal.

"Ah, we'll have a short draught, Tim. I have just a few minutes."

But that beer went down fast as Mike caught sight of the steadies and faces familiar from the sidewalk when their wedding party arrived. There were hellos and cheers to welcome him back, and Mike soon called for a second. "I'll have another if you please, Tim. Anyone else?" he asked looking down the bar. Two customers said they would, and a couple of others, who were equally agreeable, caught Tim's stern look of disapproval and said, "No thanks, Mike," and, "Another time, Mike."

Barely noticing, Mike got chatty with the couples at his sides, drank down a third, "Well, Tim, they are small aren't they?" and drove home.

Mo was relieved to see him and to enjoy his quick kiss and hug. Then, "Been drinking, Mike?"

"Well of course, Mo. Just a couple...while we're waiting. I'd pour you something, but we're all out here."

"Oh, Mike. Let's wait to celebrate, okay? There's a lot ahead of us."

"Like what, darling?" This was in the brogue, and Mo knew he was already over the line.

"Jimmy called to say goodnight, Mike. He said you promised you would be home from work. You missed him."

"Oh, that's fine. I'll go out to see him in the morning before the operation. See him at eight o'clock."

"No, Mike. Meg said the surgery has been moved up to seven o'clock, and no one can see him after midnight. How about some milk and sandwiches, Mike. Meg will call in an hour when Jimmy's asleep, okay?"

Mike followed Mo into the kitchen where she set the few sandwiches on a platter for the small kitchen table. "Did Meg leave a number for her room? Will she be sleeping where Jimmy is?"

"She gave me a number, Mike, but it will be better if you let her call you. I know you're okay, Mike; I'm just surprised. You were doing so well."

"Only because you and Meg and Jimmy have changed my life, Mo. You're my strength."

"Take my hands, Mike. Go on. Hold on to me. Now is the time for you to be strong for the three of us. Mike, you have to be strong enough for us to be *our* strength. You have to be strong enough for us to be able to lean on you—to cry on your shoulder or both shoulders. You know that, don't you, Mike?"

"Mo, it's so hard for me."

"Hard for you, Mike? Hard for you? You have to forget about you, Mike. That was your commitment when you conceived Jimmy; when he was born; when Marie died; when you married Meg. You understand that, Mike. I know you do."

"Of course. I understand. But it's hard, Mo."

"I'm not supposed to be the one who tells you this, Mike, but here goes. Booze is what makes it so hard. Booze, Mike. And beer. And wine. And as much as we love you, Mike, we can't keep going along and saying, 'Oh, it's okay, Mike, just one too many. You're over-tired Mike. Just a nice, long nap on the couch. It's okay. It's hard. We understand.' We can't keep doing that."

"Mo...I just had a couple, three draught beers this afternoon. What are you saying?"

"Don't you understand, Mike? You were 'celebrating' Jimmy's happy prognosis by drinking and thinking how good that made you feel. You. You. Not us — you! And where were you when Jimmy called you? When Meg was on the edge? You're following me on this, right?"

Then the phone rang, and Mike picked it up. "I hope this is you, Meg. Are you both okay?"

"We're okay, Mike. But we were worried; how are you?"

"I went to Phelan's, Meg; missed Jimmy's call. I don't even know how to say 'sorry' anymore. It's only nine o'clock. Will they let me in to see you and peek in on Jimmy if I drive over?"

On Mike's five minute drive to Yale-New Haven, Meg called back to

Mo and was relieved to learn Mike was just buzzed. But Mo also told her what she told Mike—he was just too selfish for his own good, in so many words, let alone the good of those around him. "I was a little hard on him, Meg. But it may help. I'm going home. Call anytime...I'll be back at the station for you from seven o'clock in the morning."

* * * * *

Y-NH Reception wasn't pleased when Mike arrived asking to be permitted up to the pre-op floor after nine o'clock, but their call to Meg persuaded them.

The two of them sat for twenty minutes holding hands, staring at Jimmy. Hugging.

"I know you want to tell me 'it's okay,'" Mike said. "And I love you for it. But it's not. I wasn't there when you called. That's my job, to be there when you and Jimmy call."

"Mike, I'm thinking only about Jimmy now. I expect you to share this challenge with me but I can't help with your challenge now, Mike. That's all your own for now."

They sat for another half-hour; it wasn't necessary to talk. It was all clear—Jimmy's operation; Meg and Mike's anxiety; Mike's recurring weakness. The sad part was that he wasn't just staggering around drunk and incapable. He was letting the 'Joy of Drinking' make everyone sad. Getting in his way—their way. Setting roadblocks that needn't be there.

They kissed Jimmy, embraced for a moment, and Mike promised to be in the waiting room at six-thirty, which is when Meg would have to let Jimmy be wheeled, alone, into surgery. They would wait together.

CHAPTER TWENTY-SEVEN

They met as agreed in the family waiting room on the operating floor—fresh and cheery—and felt some relief being together and that Jimmy's "bump" would soon be out of their lives.

"Don't you think we should let everyone know what's going on, Mike?" Neither of them had thought about calling anyone, because they never thought there would be anything to call about. Do you let relatives know about tonsils or appendix removals? How is the removal of a benign tumor any different? Do you call? If so, when? If so, whom?

So Meg and Mike were working through this as they snacked on bananas and cookies, sipped juice, coffee, and tea, sucked on peppermints, riffled through the old magazines.

By eight-thirty they agreed they should call Mike's folks, Mike and Gail, and Jimmy's grandparents, Marie's folks, Fran and Thomas, and ask them to pass the news along. This seemed to be sufficiently casual to allay any fears or anxiety while properly observing "intra-family" communication protocol, and Mike made both calls in the next few minutes.

He kept the conversations brief—his intention to downplay the seriousness of Jimmy's condition—but his admission that he and Meg were calling from the hospital raised a red flag, and both sets of grandparents were alarmed. Mike asked Meg to reassure them, and her apparent cheerfulness calmed them considerably; they promised to call all the relatives.

A bit after nine o'clock, Doctor G. came into their room with a big smile, handshakes, his endearing manner. They both felt wonderful. "Jimmy's in great shape. You should be able to see him about eleven-thirty in recovery. Sedation just makes it harder for Kindergartners to shake off the dreams, so he needs another hour or so."

Taking Meg's elbow, Bill Greenway steered the two of them through an almost invisible door panel—just next to the TV table—and into a singularly private office with coffee and mini-Danish set out on a tray table.

"Sit. Sit. Sit. Have coffee. This was a wonderful operation...all the bad stuff came out...we did a lot more scouting around to be sure...but Jimmy's fine. And he's in good shape."

"What 'bad stuff,' Bill?" Mike had heard every syllable.

"That's next, Mike. We didn't like the look of the lump root and ordered up a hurry-up evaluation on the spot. What we took out was malignant. It's okay though."

Meg and Mike stiffened and paled as one, shocked. Meg felt Mike's strong right arm around her as, leaning into him, she softly began to cry.

"Jimmy's got cancer?" Mike couldn't believe he was asking that.

"Jimmy *had* a cancer, Mike. We took it out of him. Believe me when I tell you he's in good shape."

"We believe you, Bill. Sure. But I watched Marie—that's Jimmy's mom, Bill—die after plenty of good news. She was in great shape, too. I read the papers, and I know cancer can be damn tricky, and I hope you'll be jumping beyond optimism for now and get into healing. Right?"

"Mike. Meg. I'm able to keep most of my cancer patients alive. You didn't know I was an oncologist did you? Course not, because that scares people who come in with a lump. And my little patients, well I'm ninety-four percent successful with them—more than sixteen years of doing this, Mr. and Mrs. Flynn. And my hospital put me on this case because I'm so good with people like Jimmy."

"Fine, but..."

"Just a bit more, Mike. And Meg. I don't like braggarts, and I'm not in this for the money. And Carol, my wife, and I have three great boys less than ten years older than Jimmy. I'm in this for the mommies and daddies and all their hopes and dreams. And, I'm in it for youngsters who say 'please' and 'thank you' when they get a ham salad sandwich. Any more buts?"

Mike rose, leaned over Bill Greenway, put his head next to Bill's and hugged him. Bill hugged back. Each of them was perplexed at first, then understood when all three pairs of eyes moistened on cue.

"Okay," Doctor G. said. "We can get more Danish in here but no more hankies, so let's put our 'Jimmy Plan' together. Right?"

Meg and Mike were beginning to realize as Bill Greenway and they became closer, that he had an interesting, engaging accent with unfamiliar usages—"Right?" for example, versus "Okay?" This made him all the more endearing, and when they asked him about the few teabags he kept slipping into his pocket, he said, "Brought up on it. In Australia...Sydney. Used to be coffee was too expensive down under. Least that's what my grandmam used to say. Right, mate?"

They all chuckled heartily at that, and then Mike said, "Hey, I know you. The only person who ever said, 'Right, mate' in Phelan's Pub said it when I was there. A few dopes began to boo, but I began to clap...so did everyone else. Was that you?"

"Right, mate! You made me an honorary Irishman that day. And you left without me having a moment to shake your hand. I'm shaking it now, Mike—as hard as I can. Jimmy will be fine."

CHAPTER TWENTY-EIGHT

A nurse whom Meg recognized from the night before came in just after eleven o'clock with a big smile saying, "Jimmy's fine. Let's go see him."

"Thanks for taking care of him, Barbara. Let's go. Mike, Barbara is Jimmy's special nurse, and she took good care of both of us last night."

Despite lingering drowsiness, Jimmy's eyes brightened, and he grinned at his parents as they both leaned down to hug him. "You're a tough guy, Jimmy. I love you. How do you feel?"

"Kind of hungry, Daddy. Is it time for breakfast yet?"

He frowned when they laughed but laughed when Meg said, "You've overslept, Jimmy. It's almost lunchtime. Can he have a sandwich, Barbara?"

"Anything he wants. In fact, if you can sit up by yourself, Jimmy, we'll bring some lunch in for you right now. Dr. G. tells me you like ham salad. Is that right?" It was, said Jimmy, who propped himself up in response to his nurse's challenge. "How's this?"

It was hard for Mike to control himself and, teary eyed, he pulled Meg aside. "Sweetie, this is hard. Suppose I check back at the station and meet you here at three o'clock to take you and Jimmy home. I've really got to settle down."

"Good idea. Jimmy will probably nap for an hour or two. That will be perfect. I'll let Mom know everything's fine and you're on your way."

After a short and emotional goodbye to his son, Mike did go back to his office, but it was a long drive for him thinking about the days to come. The worst was the shaved side of Jimmy's head and the wavy row of stitches in the scalp under which Dr. G. had removed the tumor. Jimmy hadn't yet realized the magnitude of the procedure and was unaware of his baldness.

Jeez, Mike thought. *What happens now? The relatives. The school kids. Will Jimmy be scared? This is going to be tough.*

Meg's call to her mother preceded Mike's arrival, and Mo had a cheery smile for him from behind the reception desk. "Jimmy's going to be okay, Mike. Sounds like Dr. G. is another guardian angel."

"We'll see, Mo. Hope so. This is hard to take."

"Oh come on, Mike. Meg said Dr. G. couldn't have been more optimistic. Sure the malignancy almost knocked me down, but don't you have to trust a doctor who remembers Jimmy's favorite sandwich?"

"You're right, Mo. You know that really impressed me. Yeah, I like him. You've got me feeling better already. Here's a kiss from your favorite son-in-law. I'll be picking Meg and Jimmy up around three o'clock. Come over to see Jimmy, and we'll have dinner together."

Back in his office, Mike's metabolism was picking up speed, then jamming on the brakes. The pink phone message slips seemed threatening. Sticky notes from colleagues cluttered open surfaces. Jimmy's situation wouldn't let him focus on the job. Dr. G's assurances and Mo's pep talk were uplifting — promising — but real?

Without a second thought, Mike stopped by Michelle's desk to say he had to catch up on some calls and wouldn't be back; that Jimmy was going home with him and Meg tonight; that complete recovery might take some time. Then he avoided Mo altogether by slipping out the back door to the parking lot and even driving his car out the rear, emergency access road. He was headed for Fitzgerald's.

A fine, much older establishment than Phelan's, Fitzgerald's was also an Irish bar, but most of its Irish customers had long since deserted to Phelan's. Once splendid, but now a bit beery and seedy, Fitz's was on Chapel Street several blocks north of The Green and directly across the street from Yale's august dormitory buildings. A carved sign above the back bar, over the old, cast-brass cash register, read, "IITYWIMWYBMAD." Over the years, thousands of regulars won drinks from "newbies" asking what the letters meant by responding, "If I Tell You What It Means Will You Buy Me A Drink," and, of course, saying, "I just told you," when the perplexed newbie still couldn't figure it out.

Now it was frequented by grad students and professors from Yale and neighborhood customers. And Mike had gone there, because very few knew who he was these days. This day the special was Guinness—rich, fresh, chewy, with a heavy head of tiny bubbles. A stout to spend time with, and Mike spent some time. And no one knew him or tsk, tsked.

The next intersection north of Fitz's was York Street, at which a left turn would bring you to the Yale-New Haven Hospital's visitors' parking area in less than three minutes, and Mike drove, parked, checked in, and met Meg and Jimmy in his room at two minutes before three. Mo was also there and only Jimmy looked happy to see his dad. "See, Mommy. See, Aunt Mo. I told you Daddy was coming."

"Begorrah. And sure enough you were right, me lad. It's me, your loving Irish daddo. How are you feeling, Jimmy?"

Jimmy clapped his hands in delight saying (in his best attempt at matching his father's brogue), "Better than ever if you don't mind, sir."

A huge hug between father and son followed Mike's up roaring approval of his son's first attempt imitating the Irish accent. "Glad to hear it, lad, now how about a kiss from these womenfolk?"

As Mike's glance focused on Meg, it passed Mo's stricken, embarrassed look at him, and Meg, smelling the Guinness, asked, "Mike, have you had lunch?"

"No lunch today, my love. Too much to do."

"Mike, you've been somewhere...some restaurant. I can smell it. A bar. What about us, Mike?"

"Well here I am. Right, Jimmy? Tell them here I am."

Meg took a step to Jimmy and lifted him into her arms. "Yes, you are here, Mike. I love you. I was praying you wouldn't abandon us."

"Never, my love."

"But you didn't come. I thought you'd be early to see Dr. G., and Mo said your car was gone. We were upset, so I asked Mom to help us out. Now I smell beer, Mike."

"Meg, I'm fine," Mike interrupted. "I'm upset, but I'm working on that. I'm sorry."

"I know, Mike. Mom will drive Jimmy and me home. Are you okay to follow?"

"Sure n' beggorah me darling."

"Mike, please. Can you drive?"

Mike realized Meg's reasonable question went beyond his behavior; his absence; his afternoon in a bar. "No, Meg. I shouldn't drive." No brogue. "Will you take me home?" He was ashamed, and no one said another thing.

CHAPTER TWENTY-NINE

The next several weeks were punishing for everyone. Mike's self pity and remorse caused a relapse that was embarrassing to Meg and Mo and to a small number of the people at Channel 5 who realized what the problem was. Tim Halloran had seen it all before and did his best by cutting Mike off after three of anything. Fitz's began seeing more and more of him.

Meg, Mo, Jimmy, and Dr. G. worked up the "Jimmy Plan," which involved chemotherapy for four weeks on, four off, four on, then measure results.

The intention was to continue with Kindergarten as long as Jimmy was holding up, and he, of course, initially enjoyed the attention his partially shaved scalp and scar caused. His classmates had secretly designed, colored, signed, and delivered a two-by-three-foot poster of encouragement and support, which went up on his bedroom wall.

As Jimmy's discomfort from his treatments began to increase, Meg persuaded Mike's boss, Dave, to let her reduce her hours to an afternoon-only schedule except for her weekly, two-hour absences for Jimmy's treatments. In the mornings, then, the school agreed to let her become Mrs. Meyer's classroom assistant. This was a non-salaried job but let Meg take care of Jimmy's special needs during regular Kindergarten hours. Some times for his aspirin or other medicine, special snacks, emergency visits to the boys' room, and also occasional, short naps in the nurse's office where he wouldn't be in the way.

Mo came back in the morning to handle some of Meg's paperwork while Michelle handled some of Meg's more sophisticated responsibilities. She was becoming uncomfortable by the increasing instances of raised eyebrows over her son-in-law's erratic office hours and more frequent absences, but she no longer felt she had any influence on him.

From the beginning, cards, flowers, and calls came in non-stop from relatives, couple-by-couple, family-by-family; Stan by himself. Generally, both Meg and Mike would be on phones to respond together, defer offers for casseroles and other meals, and postpone visits for "another few weeks."

Occasionally Mike would slur his response or would forget he'd already asked a certain question earlier in the phone conversation. This would provoke confused silences, which Meg would deal with by a clever, "Oh, we've covered that, Mike. Stop watching the ball game and pay attention."

Meg and Mo decided, after the first ten days of all the thoughtful concern they were receiving, to host a "Sandwich and Soda" luncheon the following Sunday, January 30 after the eleven o'clock Mass, at "The Flynn's Place."

Every family member seemed to be genuinely delighted with this idea—not just to visit with Jimmy and support him but to continue the family re-joining. This, of course, began on the beach at Hammonasset State Park, was reinforced at Thanksgiving, earned telephone support Christmas weekend, and peaked at the wedding. Hard to believe that was just four weeks earlier, and now rallying around Jimmy was really cementing relations with all, particularly Fran and Thomas.

January 30 turned out to be a bright, sunny day, surprisingly mild for the season, and Meg, Mike, Jimmy, and Mo unexpectedly met all the Torellis as they parked their cars in the lot adjacent to St. Vincent.

Meg, Jimmy, and Mo simultaneously shouted out greetings, which were enthusiastically echoed by Carmen and Regina. Nursing a hangover, Mike simply shrugged a greeting while Fran winced, and Thomas grimaced as though in some prostate discomfort. It occurred to Mo they were pained by their son-in-law's condition.

Spontaneously, Jimmy ran toward Fran, arms out, saying, "We missed you, Maman. But we had your famous spaghetti sauce last week. Yum. Mommy says it's magnifical."

Fran burst into tears, probably of relief, gratitude, embarrassment, then crouched to accept Jimmy's embrace. "We love you, Maman," he said, causing even bigger sobs from Fran as she choked out, "We love you too, Jimmy. All of you." And she looked up to the others.

Jimmy's innocent and genuine expression instantly nullified all the bitterness, misunderstandings, and bad manners that had contributed to the separation, and everyone broke into broad smiles, some teary, as they embraced, shook hands, and surged tightly together with Jimmy now up in Mike's arms.

They sat together during the Mass, then to visit Marie's grave on their way out of East Haven to The Flynn's Place for the luncheon. Arriving together was a singular relief for each one of them and resulted in a barrage of questions about Jimmy's treatment and prognosis, sensitive inquiries into Thomas' condition, apparently sincere best wishes over their son-in-law's marriage to Meg, and oohs and aahs over the "apartment/condo swap" and what good fortune that was.

Neither the Dickinsons nor the Torellis had ever been in Mo's lovely place, but all of them arrived and were generous in their compliments, particularly over the expansive views overlooking New Haven harbor and Long Island Sound.

Meg was glad the Torellis had arrived before the nine others, and Fran and Mo helped her with plastic cups, napkins, and party preparations. When the Dickinsons arrived, Tom and Mary with their girls, Stan Junior and the senior Dickinsons, Mary stepped in to help with the final touches.

"Have you hidden the ice somewhere besides this ice bucket?" she asked.

"Oh, for Heaven's sake, we drove right past Frank's Deli and forgot about the ice. Mike, would you get a couple bags just in case? And hurry back; it's almost twelve-thirty."

"Be right back, Meg." Mike turned to the TV room and could see Jimmy was having too much fun with Papa Thomas, so he decided not to ask them if they wanted to go along for the ride.

It was one-thirty by the time Mike got back with the ice, and he explained to Meg that Frank's was closed, and he had to go into downtown New Haven. This was a bad lie, and he knew it; Meg could smell the beer and said, "We'll talk later. Go in and welcome our guests."

The others seemed to realize what had happened and were quiet in responding to Mike's overly garrulous greetings. But Jimmy helped defuse the result of Mike's poor judgment, and all the relatives were visibly relieved to see him looking and acting so well. "A little tired I think," said Grandfather Stanhope about Jimmy. "But better than I thought he'd be."

That Fran and Thomas were so openly cordial, agreeable, and clearly just plain happy to be back with everyone, seemed a minor miracle to all. Carmen and Regina whispered explanations, as they could, that their father's prostate had been removed a few weeks before and his protracted struggle with this had been the trigger for the strange behavior.

But Jimmy was the primary focus, and all were intent on sharing time with him. It was hard for most to believe he was only in Kindergarten—he was so social and aware. And they relished his good condition, their memories of Marie, and their gratitude for Meg and her mother. Mike presented an unknown that created a curious anxiety, at best.

After the sandwiches and the sodas and the cupcakes Barbara and Martha Dickinson had brought, the natural thing for Jimmy was to use this opportunity to spread his thanks for all the Christmas gifts he'd been given. And he did this by demonstrating his familiarity and facility with all his gifts.

Stan's lovely edition of *A Visit from St. Nicholas* was the real standout...

for the obvious reasons: it was a very fancy edition with the original, color illustrations; seasonally, it was probably most apt; nearly every person attending had a loving childhood memory or other experience with it, and it appeared Jimmy was either able to read or had, incredibly, memorized large portions of it which he recited on request. And not by plain rote, but with remarkable feeling and intensity. It was an event to cherish for a lifetime, but Mike was primed to spoil it, and did.

"Hey, Stan. My son likes your fancy book, but he doesn't like sitting in your lap. And I don't either. Jimmy, come here to your dad."

Jimmy looked at his dad with an expression of complete bewilderment. "But Daddy."

Mike walked across the room, lifted Jimmy out of Stan's lap, then strode out with Jimmy still holding his book and starting to cry.

There was shocked silence until Meg said, "Excuse me," and followed her husband and son down the hall.

Stan said, "Gee, I don't know what I did. Anybody know what upset Mike?" He looked around to see his relatives shaking their heads or just staring at each other. "Well I guess I better go," Stan said. "Nice to see you all. Glad you and Thomas are here, Fran."

Meg had come out of Jimmy's room just as Stan made it to the front door, and she said, "Wait, Stan," and went out after him.

The others began to make their own signs of leaving, and Mo didn't try to persuade anyone otherwise. Fran, Mary, and a couple of the girls gathered up the plates and utensils. Mo helped those who had worn coats to retrieve them from the master bedroom.

Meg had returned quickly, could see the luncheon party was over, and also made no effort to encourage anyone to linger. She kept saying to everyone, "I'm sorry, the pressure of all this is wearing Mike down; he didn't mean anything. And Jimmy's worn out too."

The Flynn's Place was empty in just a few minutes, except for Mo, who helped Meg put away the extra sandwiches and condiments. "I don't know what to say, honey." Mo felt terribly for her daughter.

"I know, Mom. None of us do. I don't know if Mike even realizes what he said. He drank some beer you know, when he was out for the ice. It triggers a horrible reaction in him when Stan is involved in some way. He acts crazy."

"But he doesn't take it out on you, does he? He didn't seem rough with Jimmy, but he sure startled him."

"Jimmy never experienced anything like that, but he doesn't know what even a pat on his bottom is like. So he wasn't scared; just thought he'd done the wrong thing. I don't know, Mom."

"Well?" Mo probed.

"No. Mike has never, never been abusive. Just that shouting match over the flowers Stan sent. Remember?" Mo nodded. "But I should have known he'd be upset and have thrown them out myself."

Mo took Meg's hand and said, "Don't even try to accept blame for that, Meg. That's how cycles of abuse get started. Just don't think that way."

"We're back, Mommy." Jimmy and Mike were standing in the doorway to the kitchen. Jimmy with red eyes and Mike desolate and pale as a ghost. When Meg had earlier followed the two of them into Jimmy's room, all she could do was stare at Mike, sadly shake her head, then turn and walk back to the kitchen.

Now together, Jimmy and Mike walked up to Meg, and Mike put his arms around her. "I love you, Meg."

And Jimmy said, "We both love you, Mommy."

"Well that's a good start," Mo said. "See you at the station tomorrow. It was a nice party, Meg. Please try harder, Mike." She stooped to kiss and whisper to Jimmy, then left.

CHAPTER THIRTY

Over the next week Mike was unpredictably buzzed-up on beer, or partly sober, and there were sometimes flashes of the controlled Mike of not too many months ago.

Meg and Mo were working as a team to first ensure Jimmy's "Plan" was working—it was—and secondly, to do all they could to encourage and coach Mike into changing his behavior. Generally he'd spend time at his desk early in the day, return calls by leaving messages, answer his mail, pull his assignments together, and arrange his day schedule. Often he would leave the station in mid-morning to make calls and really call on his customers. Just as frequently, though, he'd return to the station high on beer and rapidly fall to a zero-productivity zone.

Dave Batchelder knew what was going on and warned Mike to turn himself around. These meetings were early in the day, and Mike was alert, committed, and determined to respond to Dave's warnings as well as his own, self-made resolutions. This wasn't working, though, and Dave decided to just let it go until Jimmy was in the clear. Then he'd probably have to fire Mike.

Two weeks after the spoiled lunch gathering, Mike and Meg were preparing for a Saturday morning visit to Doctor G. Suddenly, Mike said, "Just what do you think you're up to with Stan, anyway?"

"Stan? What do you mean?"

"I saw you rush out to talk to him at that lunch. I know exactly what you've been doing. And I've heard you whispering on the phone when you thought I was asleep."

"I rushed out to apologize, Mike. And I whisper because most of the time you're asleep and get grumpy when Jimmy or I wake you."

"Oh yeah? What about Monday night when you told me you were going over to Mo's, and when I called you weren't there, and she didn't know where you were. What then?"

"Mike, sweetie. Please don't do this; I was tired and distracted when I told you that I was going to Mom's. I meant to say I had to get Jimmy's prescription at the drug store, and I showed you the pills I picked up. I told you that. Don't you remember?"

"I'd remember that, Meg. So don't tell me this is all me; I'm not that bad. You're sneaking around with Stan. I asked you to marry me to put an end to all that—to get rid of him. You just..."

"Now listen to me, Mike. You have been drinking way too much, and you're making things up. Doctor G. told me this is delusional, and it's a symptom of alcoholism. My dad was like this. And you have blackouts and don't even remember some things that you tell me yourself. You can stop this, but you need help."

All through February these confrontations and accusations occurred regularly. Sometimes Mike would apologize; other times he would forget. Meg was on edge all the time; Mo did her best, but even Meg realized there is only so much comfort a mother can give.

At their alternate week appointments though, Doctor G. was optimistic about Jimmy's progress and his beaming, cheerful personality became an anchor for Meg. When he asked how Mike was she told him the truth, and he suggested two doctors who might be able to help—one for him and one for her—but Meg was afraid of what Mike would do if she took time to meet with one. His paranoia was growing deeper and deeper.

For Valentine's Day Meg mailed cards to Jimmy and Mike and to her mother and the girls—Carmen and Regina, Barbara and Martha. For these she altered her handwriting to look like Jimmy's and signed the cards, "Love, Jimmy," with lots of Os and Xs for hugs and kisses.

Mike forgot all about the special day, but several dozen cards arrived for Jimmy from nearly all the relatives. It was fun for Jimmy collecting them all in the few days before the actual holiday and saving them to open after their family dinner, including Mo, that night. He also sent a card to Doctor G. and had cards he'd made in school for Mommy, Daddy, and Aunt Mo.

On her way home to prepare the special dinner, Meg stopped to pick up a flower and hearts arrangement for the table and arrived just as Mo had driven up with Jimmy. "Well look what you have," said Mo. "Jimmy, show your mommy what you bought for her." As Meg peered into Mo's car from the driver's side, Jimmy held up the exact same arrangement Meg had bought. He had the biggest grin she had seen since the wedding.

"But look, Mommy, this one has heart lollipops in it, too. Daddy will really like this one."

As Mo walked behind her car to take the arrangement from Jimmy, Meg said, "Lean over here, young man and give me a kiss." And then, "Will you be my Valentine?"

"I already am," Jimmy said. "Remember—'Bee Mine 4 Ever'—like on my card for Daddy? You are mine too, right?"

"Yes I am. Now let's have a party!"

CHAPTER THIRTY-ONE

On Valentine's Day the mid-winter sun sets early enough that house lights are usually flipped on by five-thirty or six o'clock. Since either Meg or Mo was generally first to enter the Flynn's new home after work, they were both taken aback to see the lights in the hallway and living room already on.

"Hello?" asked Meg. "Is that you, Mike? Where are you?"

"Uhnn. Who's that?"

"Happy Valentine's day, Daddy!" Jimmy yelled. "Are you hiding to surprise us? Where are you?"

"Oh yeah. Here, Jimmy, I'm over here," said Mike as he sat up from his stretched-out nap posture on the living room couch and swung his stocking feet to the carpet. "What did you say?"

"Happy Valentine's Day!" Jimmy nearly screeched into his father's ear. "Will you be mine? We have lots of cards and red candy and flowers, Daddy. Don't you want to kiss Mommy and Aunt Mo?"

It was clear Mike had tumbled home to sleep off his lunchtime overindulgence. But he grabbed Jimmy for a tickling bout, and Jimmy squealed with pleasure.

"What time did you get home, Mike?" Meg asked. "We were planning a surprise for you."

"Oh thanks, honey. About twenty minutes ago, I guess. Just a little nap. Yeah, Happy Valentine's Day. I forgot."

"Thanks. Happy Valentine's Day; we've got a nice dinner planned." Meg and Mo exchanged glances, which asked the same question: Is this going to work out?

"Nice. That's nice. Let me put a fresh shirt on; be right back." Mike kissed Meg and Mo on their cheeks and headed for their bedroom; his beery, bar-smell hung in the air.

"Well, Mom, we'll do the best we can. Jimmy, let's put this bouquet on the table and the lollipops one right here in the living room, okay?"

"Sure. Where did you hide the cards? We should have them out when Daddy gets back."

Meg and Mo set out the flowers, the cards, some cheese and crackers for them, peanut butter and jelly crackers for Jimmy's snack and started on the dinner preparations. Mike was back a few minutes later and Mo had set the table while Meg put a meatloaf she had made the day before in the oven to heat up.

"What a nice idea, everyone." Mike had freshened up and seemed alert. "Wow. Look at all those cards. This is a real party."

"Look at the lollipop flowers, Daddy. I picked it out. And here's a card I made for you."

Without asking, Meg served festive cranberry juice and club soda "cocktails" to everyone, Jimmy included, and the four of them spent nearly half an hour opening and reading their cards and laughing at some of them; and assuring each other that yes, they would be their Valentines forever.

Meg slipped into the kitchen for a few minutes to bring the meatloaf, mashed potatoes, and green peas to the table and then called the others. Mo had put the place settings on red, heart-shaped paper placemats, and had lit four red candles. It was a beautiful, formal setting, and Jimmy clapped his hands with approval saying, "This is just like for grown-ups."

Meg and Mo laughed and clapped their hands along with Jimmy, then looked over, startled, to see Mike scowling at the other bouquet. "What's wrong, sweetie?" Meg asked.

"Damnit, don't you sweetie me, Meg. It's those flowers. From Stan, right? I am just so tired of him and his arrogance. When will he leave you alone and get out of my life?"

"That's enough, Mike," Meg said. "You are way out of line. Mo, will you and Jimmy excuse us for a few minutes? Mike and I need to talk."

Jimmy was wide-eyed with confusion until Mo took his hand saying, "Let's just watch one TV show, okay Jimmy?"

"These damned flowers are going right in the garbage; we went through this once, and that's enough for me. What do you see in that guy, anyway? What's the big attraction?"

"You have no idea what you are doing, Mike. What you just said makes no sense at all. It's mean to Jimmy and Mo; it's nasty to Stan, and it's abusive to me."

"Just a minute there..."

"No, Mike. I bought these flowers for us to enjoy. You can throw them in the garbage if that will help you calm down, but here is a better idea. Why don't you just go ahead and call Stan and ask him about the flowers. Go ahead—see what he says. You'll only embarrass yourself, but I'm really tired of trying to settle this thing with you. Call him. Use the phone in our bedroom so Jimmy and Mo and I can have our party."

"Damn right. I will. He's going to get a real earful." Mike grabbed the entire arrangement off the table and stomped down the hall.

Jimmy and Mo had heard Mike's part of that exchange, because he was so loud. Meg had been quiet, in control, so the complete circumstances were unclear, but they both knew it was time to eat when Mo waved them in from the TV room.

Meg brought Jimmy's lollipop arrangement from the living room, and the three of them started over. "This is good, Mommy. Why is Daddy mad at you? Because we woke him up?"

"I don't think Daddy is feeling well, Jimmy. Maybe..." and Meg was interrupted by Mike shouting into the bedroom telephone saying, "Don't try this anymore, Stan, or you'll be sorry."

"Maybe Daddy has a fever like you had before your operation, Jimmy, and needs to see a doctor. I don't know."

"I'm going out." Mike was yelling from the living room, flushed, and with perspiration on his face. "I'm going to get you your own flowers from me and a decent card. You won't be hearing from big shot Stan anymore. He's such a weakling he just hung up on me." With Meg's arrangement in his hands, Mike stomped out of the apartment and slammed the door.

Jimmy had started to call after his dad but stopped when he heard the slamming of the door, burst into tears, and ran from the table. "Let him be for a while, Meg," Mo said. "He'll get over this in a few minutes."

The two of them went back to their dinner but both were exhausted from Mike's terrible behavior and had no appetite at all. They sat silently for a few minutes, Meg hoping that Mike would come to his senses by the time he got off the elevator and would return. But she finally began to put the food back into the refrigerator.

Mo was wrong about Jimmy, and Meg found him curled on his bed, asleep. She could imagine how upset he must have been and decided to leave him until later when she could slip his pajamas on knowing he'd be sleeping soundly.

"I think we might be able to fix this at breakfast, Mom. Do you think he might have his appetite back for a special slice of cake after his corn flakes?"

"Kids are amazing after a good sleep, Meg. I'm sure he'll jump up ready to go. Might be a good idea to pack a Valentine snack for his break, though. I'm ready for a good sleep myself, honey. Call me to let me know how Mike is."

CHAPTER THIRTY-TWO

Meg waited up for Mike until after midnight, sitting up in bed trying to read, then watching television, and then dozing off. She woke when the front door banged open, and she heard him shuffling down the hall. He was drunk and, although grateful he'd been able to get home safely, she was angry. The bedroom light was off, and when he called to her she feigned sleep and heard him stagger away, probably to the couch in the living room. *Too bad,* she thought, but she wasn't ready to listen to whatever his excuse would be.

In the morning she woke him to avoid having to explain to Jimmy why he was on the couch and told him to go back to sleep in their bed. He was badly hung over. When Jimmy asked she told him Daddy was sleeping late.

Mo was right. Jimmy was full of energy, and his disappointment over the ruined party was softened by the cake and the two "bouquet lollipops" Meg put in his lunch box.

At school Meg dropped Jimmy off at his classroom and telephoned her mother from the teacher's lounge to tell her that Mike was safely home, likely to be late, and that they hadn't spoken.

Later, about ten o'clock, Mo called the school and left a message with the operator for Meg to call Mike at home. When she did, Mike was in a foul mood, wanted to know where she had been, was late for work, and needed a ride. Meg would have preferred Mike's usual poor excuses just knowing he was safe and sound, so his meanness annoyed and hurt her.

"You know I help with Jimmy at school every morning, Mike. We're having recess now. Is something wrong with your car?"

"I wanted you to drive me downtown to pick it up; I had to take a cab home last night. Can't you come and get me?"

"Mike, I have to stay with the class through lunch time, so no, I can't. And then I have to take Jimmy to daycare and put in four hours at the station. It will be much better, Mike, to call another taxi. I hope..."

Mike had hung up, and now Meg was beginning to feel a lot more assertive than she had ever been in her adult life—and resentful. She (and Mo) had done the best they could to pamper, pardon, encourage, persuade, and make excuses for her new husband whom she loved. But she was quickly realizing that alcohol dependence had made Mike a different person, and for Jimmy's sake she had to stand up to him.

And she also realized that had nothing to do with how much she loved Mike or that he might not love her. She knew that alcohol made some people act differently with those whom they love. So the test was—"Is my love strong enough and deep enough to help me pull my loved one back to again be the person I fell in love with?"

After lunch Meg dropped off Jimmy, returned to the station, updated her mom before Mo left for the day, and returned to her "paying job." Mike buzzed her intercom and said, "Happy Valentine's Day. Will you be mine?"

Meg was startled by Mike's reversal in tone from his earlier surliness and his rudely hanging up the phone but she replied, "Of course, Mike. How are you feeling?"

"You know. Beat up; angry with myself; sorry; all of it. What can I say?"

"I like the 'sorry,' Mike. What are you going to do about that?"

"Not sure, Meg. I love you. Don't know what to do." He was slurring, and in a flash Meg realized that Mike was close to being drunk again. So he must have taken a taxi to his car and then driven to Phelan's before arriving at the station, being close to falling over the edge.

"Let's go out and get some coffee, Mike. I'll drive...my car's where it always is. Now, can you do that?"

"Sure, sweetie. On my way." Meg detected a slight sarcasm but let it go when they met at her car and Mike sweetly kissed her on the forehead and opened her door for her. Both of them were silent on the short drive to The Beanery, which they ordinarily walked to.

Mike asked for ice water with his coffee and took his time with both. He kept clearing his throat and shaking his head. "Are you feeling better, Mike?" He looked pale to Meg, and she wondered if something worse than a hangover was bothering him. She almost hoped that was the case and would explain his extremely odd behavior.

Finally Mike asked, "Who was on the phone with you last night?"

"What do you mean, Mike? No one; I was waiting for you to call."

"Call? That's a laugh. I called you every five minutes for two hours and couldn't get through. Busy. Busy. Busy. Even the operator confirmed you were talking to someone. Who was it?"

"I'm telling you, Mike, I never picked up the phone. Why didn't you get in your car while you still could drive and come home and find out for yourself? This makes no sense at all."

"It makes sense to me, Meg. I told Stan he could go to Hell, and after I went out you called him to apologize. He wouldn't have the nerve to call you, so you had to call him."

This was almost too much for Meg, and she just sat there—twisting her fingers and saying nothing. Tears came to her eyes, and she did nothing about them.

Finally Mike slammed his hand on the table so hard every patron in the place jumped in alarm. "Listen to me, you. I called 946-3242 every five minutes, and it was busy." He punctuated his last word with another slam. "Don't try to tell me the phone was off the hook, because the operator told me."

Meg quietly let go and began to cry. "Oh, Mike. That's not our phone number. That was my number when I was single. We kept your number when we moved into Mom's place. Somebody else was on that phone—not me. How could you forget?"

"Let's go," Mike said. He was mortified and couldn't react any other way.

Meg spent a terrible afternoon sorting through papers on her desk and getting nothing done. She realized Mike was sinking into a deep psychosis, which she had no idea how to deal with while he was still drinking. His slamming the table really disturbed her, and she was frightened. Mo suggested she and Jimmy move in with her for a few days, but Meg declined. *It could push him deeper into the bottle*, she thought.

And that turned out to be the right decision. Mike's mistake had a profound effect on his behavior and, while they never discussed it, he seemed to recover his normal personality. Meg sensed that he was deeply ashamed, and she once again hoped this latest instance of Mike's self-debasement might mark a turn-around for him.

The next several weeks were those of mending: Jimmy's progress with Dr. G. and his treatments seemed to be working miracles; the three of them resumed attending Mass on Sundays; Mike applied himself to his work at the station and with clients; Meg gradually overcame her severe distress over the incident at The Beanery even though she didn't know whether or not Mike was drinking. But he behaved well, and she didn't really want to know.

"Just let things lie for awhile," her mom had advised, and that seemed to be best. Meg brought no flowers into their home and was careful about not whispering during her phone calls, particularly when Mike was watching television or busy with Jimmy. She answered the phone by immediately naming the caller, "Hi, Mary, how have you and Tom been?"

so that Mike's suspicions and paranoia would not be triggered.

But it was difficult, and the spontaneity was drifting out of their relationship; Mike was clearly unable to get over his problem with Stan, and it seemed to Meg that he was fixated on brooding over it.

During the cold days of March, Meg's only social enjoyment came from her conversations with Jimmy, her mother, and Mary Dickinson, with whom their new bond seemed to be growing and warming. She shared her own problems with only her mother.

In one call with Mary, Meg asked, "Isn't your birthday coming up? April 12?"

"Close, Meg. April 10—a Wednesday this year, and it's a big one, too."

"No. Don't tell me this is your fortieth?" Of course it was, and Meg expressed her surprise. "Well, you'd never know. I think people are always shocked that you're old enough for Barbara and Martha to be your daughters. How are you celebrating?"

"For years Tom has been telling me what a gala celebration he's going to put on to mark the event, but suddenly he's been strangely quiet. You know what I think that means?"

"Oh goody, a surprise party!" squealed Meg. "And a good reason to get all the relatives together. When do you think it will be?"

Mary told her she thought it had to be Saturday night, April 6, because mid-week celebrations just aren't galas, and besides, Tom would be at a law convention in Washington April 10 and 11.

"Well why don't we have lunch on Wednesday?" said Meg. "We can meet at The Solo. What do you think?"

So that was the plan, and Meg arranged with her mom to take care of Jimmy, and she let the Kindergarten teacher and daycare people know; it would be for just a few hours, and she would hardly be missed.

A few days later, Tom telephoned Mike at work, and they engaged in the usual banter and small talk. After a few minutes Tom explained his plans for Mary's surprise party, "The Big Forty," and hoped Mike and Meg and Mo could be there. "Oh I'm sure we can, Tom, and I'll check with Mo.

There are some high-schoolers in our building who will probably be able to baby-sit. Let's count on it unless you hear back from me."

Later, when Mike told Meg about Tom's call and his plans, Meg said, "Well I'm glad to hear that. Mary was sure he was planning a party but, of course, no one will tell her about it. She and I have a lunch date for her real birthday, Wednesday the tenth, but Tom's will really be fun; I'll let Mom know."

As April tenth approached, Mike's mood darkened, and Meg sensed it had to do with Stan and his presence at the surprise party. There was nothing she could do about that, and she certainly wasn't going to even mention his name let alone openly express hope that Mike would behave.

The day before the party, Mike told Meg he was going to avoid Stan and said he hoped she understood why. "I can't stand the guy. Besides, I've told you I'm jealous and for good reason. He watches you, and I know he's up to something. I'd feel much better if you just stayed out of his way." That conversation was at the station, and Mike didn't get home until past Jimmy's bedtime; he was nearly drunk and went right to bed.

Fortunately, the party was lots of fun with good conversation among all the relatives, especially Fran and Thomas, both now apparently in good health and humor. Stan was an active presence there with his date and secretary, Sarah, and the two of them spent most of their time with Mary's neighbors and non-relatives. Stan was impressing Sarah with all the people he knew. In all his conversations he was actively gesturing as he described new purchases among his antiques that the guests, he was sure, would want to own.

On the drive home Mike said, "I saw you with Stan, Meg. What did I tell you?"

"He came up to me, Mike, to introduce his secretary. What was I supposed to do, run out of the room? Really, Mike, he's harmless." And Mike let it go.

The next day though, Mike dashed to pick up the phone on the first ring of the three calls they received that day. And Meg spoke extra loudly when she called Tom and Mary to thank them for their lovely party. Mary avowed her complete surprise, and this seemed to really please Tom, who was particularly proud he had pulled it off. "I told her we were having dinner at The Solo and even made a reservation there in case she checked it out," Tom said. "She never had a clue." Before the call ended, Meg and Mary confirmed their lunch date, also at The Solo, about noon on Wednesday. Meg would make the reservation.

"What was that all about?" Mike asked after Meg had hung up. "Lunch on Wednesday?"

"I told you about that, Mike. That's Mary's real birthday, and I'm meeting her to celebrate. Tom will be out of town."

Mike frowned but didn't say another word. Meg was getting used to his dark moods, didn't like them, but prayed they would go away.

The next day at the station, Mike called The Solo and said he was Stan Dickinson calling to confirm his reservation for lunch on April 10. "That's right, Mr. Dickinson, noon this Wednesday. Still just the two of you?"

"Just the two of us, and thanks," Mike affirmed as he put down the phone, his face twisted in anger.

"I know what's going on," Mike growled to himself. "I have proof what's going on, and I'm going to catch them and put an end to it. That bastard messing around with my wife; I knew, that cheap son of a bitch. And Meg. How could you do this to us?" A lump came into Mike's throat, and he got up, walked away from the direction of Meg's office and out the door of the station. He was in Fitzgerald's for a long time.

CHAPTER THIRTY-THREE

A little after ten o'clock Wednesday morning, Meg left Jimmy at school, went home to change her outfit, then stopped by the station to check in with her mother and Mike before leaving for Farmington. She wore makeup, her hair looked great despite the drizzle outside, and she was happily looking forward to her date with Mary.

"Don't forget, Mike. Mom will pick up Jimmy at school and take him to daycare, okay?"

Mike nodded, "Sure. Have a good time, and drive carefully. Those roads are slick up there."

"Don't worry; I love you."

"And I love you," Mike said. "More than you know."

Forty minutes later Mike turned right off Route 4 onto Farmington's Main Street and immediately saw Meg's blue Taurus parked just ahead of him along the curb on his side of the street. The Solo was another fifty feet ahead on the other side of the street and, as Mike passed Meg's car, he saw the rain misting as it hit the hood, so he knew she had probably arrived right at noon.

Continuing further up the street, he stopped and backed into a space directly across from the entrance to the restaurant. And there, beneath the canopy running from the etched and beveled glass door out to the curb, was Stan's golden Jaguar.

"That prick. I'm going to scare the hell out of him." Mike felt the bile rise in his gut; his bowels began to creep, and sweat broke out on his face, neck, and chest.

Some small part of him had wanted to believe Meg and all her protestations of innocence, and he had held out a slither of hope that she was telling him the truth. Now he knew. "Oh, Meg, I tried so hard."

The adrenaline began to pulse in him as he pulled the revolver from under his seat and checked to ensure he had taken out all the bullets and left them in his dresser at home.

I've got all day, he thought, and he took the pint of Scotch out of the center console and swallowed another ounce. He had already consumed about a third of it on his drive from New Haven, but the adrenaline push was stabilizing the alcohol's effect on him, and he wanted more.

The rain continued in varying levels of intensity, every now and then turning into a drenching downpour for up to a minute. It beat on his car and on the windows, and he could hardly see across the street. When this happened he would lower his window to eye-level to be sure no one leaving the restaurant escaped his notice.

Mike waited for nearly an hour, at one time nearly bursting into tears with the hurt and rage he felt over Meg's infidelity. The gun rested between his thighs, and he continued to take occasional sips of the Scotch.

And then he saw them come out of the restaurant. They were both bent over, Stan leading the way to open the door to his car. "That's my wife, you bastard," Mike hissed. Mike couldn't see Meg's face, but she'd see his after he'd reduced her lover to a quivering coward pleading for forgiveness.

Stan slammed the passenger door shut and moved around the front of his car to ascend the curb as Mike threw open his own door and got out. He stood in the street with the raised gun in his right hand and his right forearm steadied on the top of his door as he tracked Stan.

At that moment another deluge of rain began pounding down, and Millicent Payson, the 81 year-old retired librarian from the Farmington Public Library, pressed the down button for her side windows so she could see more clearly. Her cataracts usually weren't much of a handicap, but a misted windshield combined characteristically with her clouded eyes to severely limit her vision. Millicent erroneously thought that an open window helped with de-misting.

She was headed slowly up the street toward Mike when he shouted out, "It's over, Stan."

Stan looked up and was galvanized by what he saw. It couldn't be. He screamed back, "Mike. No!" and Millicent turned her head in Stan's direction and lost all sense of where she was headed.

In the next instant, the front of Millicent's car slowly pushed against Mike, squeezing him into his opened door and then crushing both Mike and the door to the pavement.

Startled by the odd resistance she felt, Millicent braked to a stop and now saw Stan dash past her shouting, "Stop! Stop!" as he ran to Mike. He knelt and lifted Mike's head in an attempt to stem the blood gurgling up from his lungs and throat. Kneeling next to Stan was Sarah, who had run after Stan and now broke into sobs when she realized who it was. Struggling, she asked, "What did you want, Mike?"

Mike heard her and turned his head saying, "You, Meg. I wanted you." Then he opened his eyes, realized his mistake, and dropped into a coma.

Stan said to him, "Hold on, Mike. Just hold on." And he took the revolver from Mike's hand and put it in his raincoat pocket.

EPILOGUE

It was years before I knew about that terrible event. In fact, I learned the truth just yesterday from my "Uncle" Stan Dickinson, who had been the unsuspecting target of my father's rage outside The Solo restaurant in the cold, wet drizzle on Farmington's Main Street that awful April day. I had graduated from Yale the week before, and Uncle Stan and I were having a celebratory and farewell lunch at Mory's. Now I'm on a train to Newport, Rhode Island to begin Officers' Candidate School, with the expectation of being commissioned a naval officer in a few months.

Uncle Stan has always been generous, and he sent me off with an envelope stuffed with twenties—$1,000 in all—packed in the bottom of one of the bags my mother and father had with them on their Bermuda honeymoon. Newport is just a couple of hours from New Haven, and both my mother and Uncle Stan wanted to drive me right up there and onto the naval base. But I couldn't bear the thought of going mushy in front of the other hundred or so OCS candidates also arriving.

So we agreed to a handshake, a big hug, kisses, and just a bit of slobbering on the train platform in New Haven, from which I took the Amtrak to Providence, the station closest to Newport.

And I must admit, despite going off alone, I teared up anyway after I got on the train. What Uncle Stan had told me about my father was painful to learn. Also, I knew I would miss the laughter, hugs, kisses, "atta boys," and other forms of praise that had surrounded my life. So many around me loved me, and I loved them back.

For my Italian birth mother, Marie, family was everything, and Italian children were even more if that's possible. I only had her arms around me for a few years, but it was enough to ensure her family values stuck to me. She made life as cozy for me as my first friend, Fluffy, whom I slept with and left on my mother's grave. That was to get Fluffy up to Heaven to keep her company.

My 'growing up' mother, Meg, and her mother, whom I called Aunt Mo, were Irish like my father, Mike Flynn. Their family values were as strong and important as Marie's but expressed differently. My Italian relatives showed family love by laughing, dancing, and with strong, steely emotions. The Irish relatives joked more, kidded more, cried more, and hugged and kissed all the time. And, as I learned watching my father, crashed hard too—and not just when vehicles were involved.

My father didn't die in the crash that April day. He was horribly injured and spent months in a coma, then months more in rehab. But that crash was the explosive end of a self-destructive path he had been walking a long time. The aftermath of it was a terrible time for everyone, but most particularly for me, because I couldn't understand what had happened. After all, who would ever tell a first-grader his drunken father had flashed a revolver at his brother-in-law and been struck and almost killed by an elderly driver?

Yesterday at Mory's, I was aghast at Uncle Stan's explanation of what had taken place. At the same time I was glad that I hadn't known about it before. When I recovered from the shock, I asked why my father hadn't been sent to jail. Uncle Stan said he had told the police it was a family misunderstanding and that Mike Flynn was his brother-in-law, drunk, and psychotically suspicious that he and my mother were having an affair.

There was some confusion about whether or not my father had pointed a gun, none was found, and in depositions no one could—or would—say for sure. So no charges were made.

My mother, of course, had been hysterical when she and Aunt Mary came out of The Solo and saw her crushed husband bloody and unconscious in the street with Stan and his secretary, Sarah, bending over him. Thank God, really, that Aunt Mary and Uncle Stan were there to help her.

I didn't know what happened, but I recall those dark, cold April days and worried looks instead of smiles on everyone's faces with low voices murmuring. I wasn't getting the attention I was used to and was certain I was somehow connected with the reason my father wasn't around.

I was still being treated by Doctor G., who was doing all he could to ensure that the cancerous tumor I had wouldn't return. This meant visits to his office, day trips to the hospital for treatments and, for a while, pills that made me sick. All that time I expected to see my father in one or another of the hallways or patient rooms, waiting for me, but I never did. Only once did I ask why he wasn't there. My mother and Aunt Mo both began to cry, so I never asked again.

At Christmas time my father finally came home, and my heart nearly burst with the love I felt for him. That feeling came back every Christmas afterwards, and it was wonderful for me. My mother and Aunt Mo and I were all excited and had a tree and presents and lights all set up. My father was very thin, and he walked a little bent over, but his laugh was the same, and he told some jokes in his Irish brogue. If he laughed too hard he would cough and have to stop laughing.

On Christmas Eve my father asked where Uncle Stan's book was, *A Visit from St. Nicholas*; how happy I was to cuddle up to him on his big chair by the tree as he read the story to me. At the end he said, "Jimmy, Santa Claus always comes back just before Christmas like I have, but don't worry, I don't plan to go away any more. I was sick, but I'm better now."

We all went to Mass Christmas day, and afterwards my Torelli and

Dickinson relatives came over for turkey and presents. Everyone was very careful to not bump into my father, and he made a joke about that and laughed, but no one else did. Finally, I laughed too. I didn't know what the joke was about, but I was so happy to see my father and to hear him joking around again. Then everyone else joined in.

After that we slowly eased into our old routine, with my father and mother going back to work and Aunt Mo watching out for me after school. My father tired easily, and my mother wasn't really her old self. She didn't laugh as much or tickle me. Once, I was helping Aunt Mo dry the dishes after dinner, and when I dropped and broke a glass, my mother came running into the kitchen, and I was frightened. She was too, and she held me for a long time saying it was okay, over and over.

The next Valentine's Day was good for everyone. My mother and Aunt Mo were relaxed and cheery, and so was my father. I brought home from school some cards given to me by my classmates and cards I had made for my family. I also had made a lollipop tree like my mother had bought the year before. I remembered how I had cried when I woke up that morning and the tree and lollipops were gone. My mother had told me they gave my father a headache.

But the main reason everyone was cheery was that Doctor G. told us my cancer was gone, and I probably wouldn't get any more bumps on my head or anywhere else, and I never did.

I saw Doctor G. every year after that for some time, and he was always happy when we came in, and he always had a ham salad sandwich for me. When he asked about my father, sometimes my mother would smile and share good news, and some years she would shake her head and frown.

Soon after that Valentine's Day, my mother and father and I went to my birth mother's grave site to leave flowers. It was always nice for me to see the little angel on that nearby headstone, and I liked those visits, but this year turned out to be different.

After we got home, my father went out for a long time. I remember how upset my mother became when he finally returned, laughing and joking and talking in his brogue. She cried, and then they yelled, and in the morning my father was sleeping in the living room.

That afternoon he and my mother told me he was sick again and had to go away. Aunt Mo was going to drive him, and before they left he said, "I know I promised, Jimmy, but I'll be okay and miss you, and I'll come home soon." He cried a little bit, and I hugged him harder, and he hugged me back.

That time he did come back soon—after only a few days. But as the years went by he left more frequently and stayed away for weeks at a time. Finally, no one talked about it or explained much. They told me he was sick again but not like I had been sick. It was strange to me, but finally I came to realize, or was told, that my father was an alcoholic. Beginning to understand what that meant helped me to shake off the self-blame and guilt.

Over time, I began to consider him as another relative, not as my father and my mother's husband. And after a while it didn't bother me much, because my mother was at her best when he was away and for the first few days after he returned. We just slowly adjusted to this, and it was never the same again, and we all suffered by his illness and behavior.

The shock comes at you out of the blue when you suddenly recall one of your father's good days, one of the good old days, and you realize these are gone—have been gone.

The shock hits you when you recall waiting until Christmas Eve to buy your tree, and when you got to Charlie's corner lot he had set one aside for you; and he had hot chocolate, too! That magical event slowly drifts away when your father just doesn't feel like it.

You remember the short drives to visit your mother's grave after Sunday Mass and often meeting the Torellis there. It's different when your father can't get out of bed in the morning. You still go, but the feeling is like the day you spotted rust on the shining chrome wheels of your new, two wheeler bicycle.

The tickles stop; the race to the shower; buying flowers together for your mother; trying to improve your own Irish brogue; Carmen and Regina not babysitting anymore, because your mother and father no longer go out for dinner.

You are startled to sense that so many of the little things holding a family together have just faded away. Startled because these little things are the sparks that kindle the love that glows inside the loving, caring, healthy family. You walk into the kitchen one morning, and the glow has gone. The kidding, the praise, the care...even the hope has given up.

As you get older and into high school and become more aware of your father's problem and what it does to others, you realize that his alcohol is drowning out those little sparks of love.

Uncle Stan would visit during my father's absences, and in time we all became closer and closer. When my father finally died ten years later, in my sophomore year of high school, Uncle Stan was a tremendous help to me—and to my mother—in getting us through it. Eventually he became my guide and mentor.

With my mother's and Uncle Stan's insights, I finally came to see that my father just couldn't help himself. He loved us all, and he tried as hard as he could, but it was beyond him. His alcoholism and the residual pain from the car hitting him drove him down into depths from which he could not crawl out. Uncle Stan told me it also probably had to do with the early death of my birth mother, and I remember thinking, even as a child, how hard that must have been for him.

Although my father's death was tragic, now my mother is happier, and our lives have been good. She still works at Channel 5. Aunt Mo remained retired and lives with my mother in her old apartment, The Flynns' Place.

So now I'm on the train to Providence, where a college classmate and his dad will pick me up and take me to Officers' Candidate School. Since I went to college just five minutes away from both my mother and Aunt Mo, this will be my first real break from home. As I head toward my new life, I keep thinking of the one I'm leaving, the one shaped by my birth mother, my growing-up mother, and my father. I miss him still. He always tried hard but was too weak to fight off his own demons. These are the demons that snared him in one or another of his gin mills where he'd forget about the baseball game we were going to, or my Cub Scout meeting, or the birdhouse he and I planned to make for Mother's Day.

When he was trying he was a good, decent man who loved my two mothers and Aunt Mo and me. I loved him back, and I know from my mother and Uncle Stan that my love helped him.

One more thing I keep remembering. After Uncle Stan told me at lunch about that awful April day, I asked where my father got the gun. My uncle looked away for a few moments then turned back to me with solemn, baleful, misty eyes. He said, "From me, Jimmy. He saw it in my antique shop one day; it was an old, Colt 1851 Navy revolver, and he admired it. Earlier I had made a mistake in my relationship with him that I never got over, and neither did your father. I gave the gun to him as an apology and having that gun enabled him to terrify me and was the beginning of his end."

Later, as I was packing to leave, I asked my mother if she knew what Uncle Stan meant when he told me he had made a mistake with my father. She looked perplexed for a moment, shook her head, relaxed into our old hugging routine, and said, "No idea."

I said, "I'll always be your Valentine, Mom."

She said, "Be safe. Be mine. I love you."

And that's my story.

ABOUT THE AUTHOR

A former advertising executive, John McCurdy lives in central Connecticut with his wife, Kathy. They have three grown children.